A CERTAIN
MR. TAKAHASHI

ANN IRELAND

A CERTAIN MR. TAKAHASHI

~ a novel ~

SIMON & PIERRE FICTION
A MEMBER OF THE DUNDURN GROUP
TORONTO · OXFORD

Printer: Webcom

National Library of Canada Cataloguing in Publication

Ireland, Ann
A certain Mr. Takahashi / Ann Ireland.

ISBN 1-55002-456-6

I. Title.

PS8567.R43C42 2003   C813'.54   C2003-905012-2

1   2   3   4   5   07   06   05   04   03

THE CANADA COUNCIL | LE CONSEIL DES ARTS
FOR THE ARTS | DU CANADA
SINCE 1957 | DEPUIS 1957

Canada

ONTARIO ARTS COUNCIL
CONSEIL DES ARTS DE L'ONTARIO

We acknowledge the support of the **Canada Council for the Arts** and the **Ontario Arts Council** for our publishing program. We also acknowledge the financial support of the **Government of Canada** through the **Book Publishing Industry Development Program** and **The Association for the Export of Canadian Books**, and the **Government of Ontario** through the **Ontario Book Publishers Tax Credit** program, and the **Ontario Media Development Corporation's Ontario Book Initiative.**

Care has been taken to trace the ownership of copyright material used in this book. The author and the publisher welcome any information enabling them to rectify any references or credit in subsequent editions.

J. Kirk Howard, President

Printed and bound in Canada.
Printed on recycled paper.
www.dundurn.com

Dundurn Press
8 Market Street
Suite 200
Toronto, Ontario, Canada
M5E 1M6

Dundurn Press
73 Lime Walk
Headington, Oxford,
England
OX3 7AD

Dundurn Press
2250 Military Road
Tonawanda NY
U.S.A. 14150

Acknowledgments:

Thanks to the following for editorial advice during the long life of this manuscript: Cynthia Holz, Juli Trapp (Amaro), Cathy Ford, Bill and Tekla, Tim, and Margaret Woollard.

Grateful acknowledgment is also made to Warner Bros. Inc. for permission to quote from "Steel Rail Blues" by Gordon Lightfoot, ©1966 Warner Bros. Inc. All rights reserved.

Chapter One

When I was sent upstairs after singing a sudden brilliant chorus of "God Shave The Queen", Colette knew what to do. My bedroom was on the third floor facing the street, so it was natural to perch on the sill and look out at what I was missing. The laughter of children echoed louder and gayer than ever. Across the road, Yoshi Takahashi's black Thunderbird lay sleekly in the driveway. He had already been out once during the day and had returned packing a mysterious blue box.

Suddenly, there was my sister, Colette, on the sidewalk, calling up through the funnel of an empty toilet-paper roll.

"Je-ean!" she sang, a clear soprano.

Delighted, we chatted, finding much to say from the new perspective. After a time Colette got a crick in her neck so, hold on, I tossed a blanket out the window, then a pillow. Spreading both on the cement she lay down, delicately resting her head on the pillow. It was nearly perfect. Soon I devised a system of passage: the long string from my kite was knotted around the window frame and tied to a basket, and before long I was lowering comic books, MAD magazines, pencils, and paper, anything to keep her with me. For a time we were quite silent, like two children lying side by side on the rug solemnly colouring.

Then I had a brief, sharp thought. Was she lying there hoping Yoshi would emerge from his house, perhaps to mail a letter or put out the garbage? Would he see her lying there and wave her over for a visit? I, of course, would be trapped above, able to do nothing but watch.

There were three short tugs on the string. I hoisted up the basket and unfolded the little note.

"I have a *plan!*" it said.

I nodded and looked down. Colette had pushed aside the blanket, pillow, and magazines and lay awkwardly sprawled on the bare pavement. We waited for a car to pass.

Sure enough, this being a "family" street, the first car slowed down, animal-like, and the driver leaned out the window.

"You okay?"

Not a sound. Not a muscle stirred.

"Hey, kid, anything wrong?"

The car nosed its way to the curb. Sensing the moment, Colette stood up slowly and, like a sleepwalker or a ghost, slid inside the house. All done with exquisite control. Meanwhile, from my bleacher seat I was clapping and laughing my guts out. Colette counted to twenty or so – until the car had taken off down the street – then came out again. Once more she fell crumpled on the sidewalk, to await the next victim.

Suddenly, to my horror, the yellow door across the street swung open. Yoshi stepped outside, a thick score tucked

8

under an arm, and turned to lock the door. He skittered down the cement stairs two at a time in his bright red sneakers, watching Colette all the way.

She snapped to a sitting position, palms flat against the pavement.

"Hello, how are you?" He waved the score in the air.

"Fine, I'm fine!" she returned. Her back was twisted so I could only hear the smile in her voice.

For a moment I was sure she was going to get up and follow him, a sleepwalker still, into the black Thunderbird.

Leaning out the window of my crow's nest I began to signal wildly: "Hello, hello!" but my salute was collared by a gust of wind and vanished without a trace.

Soon the car door crunched shut, and the Thunderbird cruised lazily down the street like a black beetle, sunlight glinting off its rear window.

Colette began gathering up her things, making a little pile of the blanket, pillow, magazines—everything I'd ferried down. She didn't send them back up in the basket. Instead she hoisted them inside the house like a sack of laundry, leaving only a comic book to flap on the curb.

□

Sun and street noise blast through the windows on the west wall. The Bowery is waking up.

Jean winds around the loft, blinking in the sunlight. Her bare feet pick up bits of dust and straw from the unswept *tatami*. She is cradling a bowl of steaming tea in her hands. As she passes the open window a summer breeze floats in, rippling the light cotton of her kimono. Someone below tosses a bottle to the pavement where it shatters noisily.

She stops for a moment. Lying on the low table is a sheet of paper torn from a pad. It reads:

Jean: The enclosed may be amusing. Please promise you will be there.

9

"I am not yet Okakura – I am
But his ghost shaped by the sound
Of your prayers."
Love, Colette.

Jean kneels to read the enclosed clipping. She slips the
tea cup under the table onto the little shelf.
"THE IRREPRESSIBLE SAMANTHA KRAUSS"
This headline is strung over a smudged photo of Sam,
their mother, who is perched on a low stone wall. A striped
sailor shirt stretches across her ample bosom. Her features
are blurred but recognizable.

Between teaching sessions, Victoria's pre-eminent vocal
teacher, Samantha Krauss – or Sam Hopper – as she is
known to intimates, is very much a family woman.
"In my next life I'm going to be the world's best
housewife!" she declares, and passes her guest a potent
Bloody Caesar. We are sitting on the patio of her delightful new home, designed by renowned Vancouver
architect, Derek Arthur. Very much on Miss Krauss's
mind these days is the gala celebration she and her husband, Martin Hopper, plan to commemorate their move
into the new home. After twenty years in Toronto they
made their Western odyssey last year.
Mr. Hopper, raised in London, is a former student of
the Viennese cellist Leopold Auer, and plays cello in the
Styles-Hopper Quartet, in addition to his duties as Acting
Dean of the Faculty of Music –

Etcetera. Jean settles into a loose half-lotus and skims
on:

"This party serves a dual purpose," Miss Krauss explains. "Besides being a celebration of Mr. Arthur's magnificent achievement, my husband has a very special
announcement to make." This statement is accompanied

10

by a mischievous smile. "We are about to start a new chapter in our lives . . . "

Jean's eyes glaze over. It's the first she's heard of any announcement. She squirms and flexes her toes, trying to bring some life to them. She feels faintly disappointed that her name wasn't mentioned—"arriving from New York City is daughter Jean . . . "

"Please promise you will be there," writes Colette, natural as can be. Damn sure she's pulled it off.

It was exactly six weeks ago. Jean's twenty-second birthday.

"Let me take you to an off-Broadway show," her friend Reuben had insisted. The show was only so-so, but afterwards they strolled through the crowded streets laughing, trying to remember the songs, cooking up new, sillier lyrics.

"Where do you want to go now?" he asked.

"CBGB's," said Jean instantly.

The cab dropped them at the entrance on Bowery, which was pulsing with loud music and a mob of underage teenagers fighting to get in.

"Sure?" asked Reuben. His hand slid to his pocket.

"Yes."

The sign on the front screamed in foot-high letters: "MAX ROMEO AND THE WILD SINS OF MEXICO."

"Okay, let's go in." Reuben pushed the door open.

A fat man perched on a stool slid a hand out.

"Five bucks, kids."

Reuben paid up, and they pushed their way through the mass of twitching bodies toward the stage area.

The band was pounding a syncopated Latin rhythm as Max Romeo, dressed in baggy white ducks and a Hawaiian shirt, belted into a hand-held mike. Sweat poured from his hair onto his hands. Jean watched, transfixed, almost missing Reuben's urgent gesture.

11

"I see two chairs!" he mouthed into the racket.

An elbow dug into her ribs, and she bounced off a glassy-eyed girl who was shaking green sparkles out of her hair.

Reuben had clamped his hands over the back of a couple of folding chairs.

Jean bopped over to him, tipping side to side with her hips, sliding her sneakers over the wet floor.

Just for an instant she worried, "Will this destroy my ears?" Then, to hell with it, she cakewalked into his arms, forcing him to dance with her. His paint-stained fingers meshed with hers as he allowed a quick vamp around the table. Then he shouted near her ear, "I'll get beer!"

She nodded.

As he disappeared into the crowd she hung tight, watching the band and keeping an arm hooked through the chairs.

Max Romeo was beautiful – all sharp lines and slippery skin, his pelvis a Mexican jumping bean trotting all over the stage. She scanned the audience that pressed near him, bruising the lip of the stage with their hips and sweat. There was no room to actually dance. Instead, people hopped in place, except for a group of cool loners who leaned to one side, smoking and sipping tepid beer.

Suddenly Jean's eyes riveted on the spot directly beneath Max Romeo. The stage lights had picked out two shapes from the others. The couple had their backs to her at first, but soon spun so their profiles jutted into the smoky haze.

The man was older than the woman, his thick hair sprinkled with grey.

The floor began to shift under Jean's feet.

"It can't be," she whispered, the dense air hugging her nostrils.

He was dressed all in black. Small and wiry, he moved in neat, quick snapshots. The woman was thin, taller, and danced with self-conscious gestures – an arm lashing toward the ceiling, her neck whipping back and forth like a snake.

12

Jean felt a soft pressure on her elbow. Reuben. Without looking, she groped for the cold beer.

Reuben followed her stare.

"Isn't that the famous pianist . . . ?"

"Yes!" she snapped, before he could fill in the words, the name.

There was an explosion as the drummer thrashed his high-hat, his teeth clenched around a wad of gum, and Max Romeo bent and squirmed and finally shrieked into the mike, sending the room into a frenzy of vibration.

The couple was hidden in the activity, lost in the wave of bodies that rushed the stage. Frantically ducking the sea of elbows and shoulders, Jean backed against the wall.

With a final cymbal cheer, the song was over.

The room gasped for breath.

Then Jean saw them again. A flash of black and red as the young woman fell exhausted into the man's arms. Laughing, he held her there, rubbing the small of her back and, at the end, lifting her head so he could reach her lips.

Jean felt the beer toss out of her hand onto the front of her jeans. A welcome splash of cold.

"Are you okay?" Reuben was right there.

"No," she said. "We must go."

Six weeks ago. Jean forces herself to run the scene through yet again, a government agent studying the moment of connection, the passing of secret information.

First there is the thatch of black hair falling over the broad moon face, the collar open and loose, the arm reaching up to Colette's neck, touching – no, caressing – her skin. The tenderest laugh imaginable.

Could she have been mistaken in the dim light, the murky air of a bar on a hot evening?

She'd know his profile anywhere, and Colette's – two in the world she'd never mistake. The light stamped them into a grey cut-out on the wall.

13

□

It was a crazy ride, Colette. There's still a breeze in the air; you can't deny it.

He landed in our neighbourhood like a gymnast from an Elysian trapeze, carrying the smell of jasmine, green tea, and five years of our lives.

The windows were wide open. It was late October, and the streets were littered with fiery maple leaves and remnants of the Sunday paper. Beethoven's Piano Concerto No. 3 suddenly crashed into our house – through the walls, into our living-room – vibrating our tender eardrums. It came from the grandest of pianos – Yoshi Takahashi's. His tightly manicured fingers dashed over the keys, sinking, then springing with athletic bounce to the next chord. Our new neighbour. There were hints of his good looks – our mother's smile and overheard conversations – and we even saw him once as he dashed the short distance from his black T-bird to the yellow door of his house, 115 Dundeen Square. Our neighbour! World famous, not quite thirty years old, and perhaps (dare we imagine?) *lonely* in a new city. Did he speak English? We asked around. Some. He spoke Music, the word that was still a mocha cream in our hearts, a bleeding centre of dissolving sensuality we were so eager to swallow.

One Sunday afternoon in the winter, when no one was home but us, we opened the living-room window wide so the air blasted a clear current from his house to ours, then cranked up the hi-fi so it filled the sub-zero wind with the latest Rolling Stones – and he knew we were hip. We were in this together, Colette, not a dime's worth of separate thought between us as our eyes gleamed anticipation. We plotted to meet him.

"Let's bake a cake!" I cried in a moment of inspiration. "We can take it over as a welcoming gift."

"What kind of cake?" Colette eyed the pantry shelf.

Gripped by a sudden, delicious image I scooped out two boxes of Betty Crocker mix and dropped them on the counter.

"A *piano* cake!"

It took hours mixing and baking, then cutting one layer of Devil's Food cake into ladyfingers for the black keys. The other layer we shaped into the piano body – baby grand, aerial view. White cake became the white keys, and everything was glued and glazed with icing.

"It's beautiful!" we sang, staring at our shiny sculptured feat, a Liberace-lush edible piano. Yet when it came time to wrap it in foil and hunt up an Eaton's box the proper size, I was suddenly seized with terror. Who were we after all? Twelve and thirteen years old, ungainly adolescents with a pagan offering to our chosen god. Colette urged us on, seeing no obstruction to the unfolding drama. He'll slam the door in our faces, I imagined. Or laugh. Or bow politely, *then* press the door shut in our faces. Oh, Colette. Oh, Jean. We hugged each other breathlessly before setting out to the cool cement walk.

He wasn't home.

Funny, the car was there. Perhaps he was working. We didn't quite know what to do, though I was vastly relieved. Colette wanted to take the box home and go back later, but no, I said, let's just leave it on the doorstep with a note. Okay, what shall we write? I pulled out a piece of paper, flattened it against Colette's back, and printed: "PLEASE EAT THE PIANO. Jean & Colette (your neighbours)."

Was that good enough? All right, Colette said, and we stuck it under the box and left it on the mat. Later in the afternoon we looked over and the box was gone.

"He's taken it!"

"Maybe he's eating it right now!"

The thought of him at that moment crunching down on our home-baked cake incited giggling, a fit that lasted on and off till bed-time. We knew we were stepping into the shallow water of a miracle.

Later, another evening, we had tickets to his concert with the symphony. Tickets that came from a benevolent relative, pleased to see our excitement for the "classics". The music we half listened to; it was the spare shape of him there, balanced against the gleaming black Steinway with his dark eyes focused artfully inward that we clung to, our heads pressed against the brass rail of the second balcony. Each time he tossed his head or plunged his arms into the black-and-white nest of keyboard, Colette jiggled my elbow.

"Look at him!" we squealed, sometimes so noisily that our neighbours, serious music students following scores, scowled, even put their fingers against pinched lips. What did we care!

When it was over and he had bowed, accepting with gracious humility the shouted "Bravos" and accompanying ovation (in which we participated lustily and I felt hot tears, leakage from my inner self, brush down my face), we headed for the greenroom. We were determined to meet the Dream head on. In the corridor, our heads bobbed up and down in the sea of adults.

"I see him!"

"He's coming out of the room!"

"His hair's drenched in sweat!"

We watched as, one by one, he shook hands with friends, vague acquaintances, strangers. Up close his face was large, moonlike, and dark. We could see grey hammocks of fatigue slung under his eyes. It was our turn. With red, beaming faces we introduced ourselves.

"We live across the street from you. Remember the box of cake . . . ?"

Then there was the explosion, and Colette and I were at the centre. His strained face broke into a delighted smile as he gathered us into his kimonoed arms.

"Ahhh. The piano cake girls."

16

What a beginning! Our smiles stretched to breaking and rocketed off our faces into the world. He told us to stay back so he could drive us to the party at his house. Moments later we were there, dropped from the everyday blandness of our household into the exotic temple of his world, a house paved in white carpets, with huge pillows on the floor like beds, wine and cigarettes, the laughter of musicians, the heady smell of success—and us. We were whisked to the middle of it, as if he'd been waiting all along.

◻

What colour is betrayal? muses Jean. Purple?

She packs her suitcase, tossing in underwear, a toothbrush, a change of jeans.

She passes again Colette's short note fluttering on the table, ghost of Okakura, the handwriting spidery and familiar. And passes, too, inevitably, the cello standing in the corner, its side swung toward her.

"Off again in such a hurry?" it mutters.

When she doesn't reply, it adds, "The humidity's terrible. Can't you hear my pegs creak in the night?"

"Yeah, I hear them," says Jean, stuffing a handful of socks in her suitcase and looking around for her toilet kit.

"It's been over a month." A sigh. "I'm nothing like this. A sculpture? You could at least dust me from time to time."

"Shut up!" says Jean.

She could lock it in the case and shove it in the closet. That might shut it up.

"Poor old neglected thing," she says, with a hint of bitterness. Has she ever gone six weeks without picking up the bow?

She folds a blouse into the suitcase, pats it down, then sighs heavily. Grabbing the chamois that drapes off a tuning peg, she wipes it over the rosewood soundboard. Hardly dusty at all. She can almost hear the purr of contentment. This annoys her. She feels slightly queasy, almost motion-sick, as she flips the instrument around to swipe its underside. She shakes the chamois and tosses it into the open case. Before she knows it, she's tightening the bow and passing the horsehair over a knob of resin. She unscrews the endpin and sticks it into a crack in the floorboards. Then she drops the bow on the string and draws it across tentatively.

A muted sound, like an infant crying two floors away.

She cocks her head, listens, and does it again. Then her left hand springs to the fingerboard, and the sounds turn into a familiar transcription: a Bach partita. Her fingers nimbly follow the old pattern, and the bow stabs at the proper angles.

She plays ten or twelve bars before stopping in disgust.

"What crap!" She glares at the instrument before propping it up against the wall again.

Her fingers work by habit: might as well be raking leaves. How long since she's actually listened? Might as well be a civil servant plowing through scores of documents and procedurals.

She slides the suitcase toward the door, ready for a hasty exit in the morning.

Colette doesn't know Jean has quit playing. No one in the family knows. Jean wonders how she'll tell them.

◘

One day, the last summer the family was together at the cottage, Sam said, "Let's go pick raspberries."

"Sure," we said, thinking of pie and waffles.

Then Father called, "You stay here, Colette, and help me bring in the dock."

When we got to the field, the farmer gave us each pails that fastened around the waist.

As we picked, Sam did the talking.

18

"Your father and I aren't entirely happy about your plan to go to New York."

I started to pick too fast, squishing berries as I slid them off their stems.

"Martin isn't sure that you'll like it there. The city is extremely competitive . . . "

"I know that!" I snapped.

She sighed. "And apart from anything else, it's expensive. If you really want to get away from home, how about Queen's? That's where I went. You could come home weekends."

I didn't say anything. A bee tried to get up my sleeve.

Finally she came out with it: "Your decision doesn't have anything to do with Yoshi, does it?"

He was living in New York, had been for months.

I slammed the berry into the pail. I was making a terrible mess.

"No!" I was furious. Did she think I would place my future on the line—my career, the next chapter of my life—for him? A childhood infatuation?

"That's not the reason at all!" I cried.

Maybe he'd given the name "New York" a shimmer. Like Hemingway or Piaf in Paris. A certain aura. And sure it would be easier to keep up with his doings if I could check out the papers every day. But what was the chance of running into him in a big city like New York? Would our paths intersect? Pretty damn unlikely. And would I look him up on my own? I didn't know yet.

"For music, New York's still the place," I said.

Sam sighed. "I want to be sure of your motives. And sure you're sure." Her pail was filling efficiently. "If I knew you weren't on some wild goose chase after that man I'd feel a lot better. So would your father." She gave me a hard look. "Even Colette is worried."

"I'm not chasing anyone," I said. "I just want to play the cello."

I even believed it.

19

Chapter Two

I don't know whether to fear
Or love you, ghost.

Does Colette have laugh and frown lines about her eyes
now? From holding expressions too long? We're old Ka-
buki actors posing a dramatic *mie*, crossing one eye over
the other for the thousandth time.

◘

Jean steps off the ferry onto the Victoria dock. It was a
rough crossing, and she sways for a minute, holding on to
the suitcase. A gust of wind sweeps across the concrete
and billows her blouse into a tent. She squints at the little
crowd of welcomers.

A horn bleats a sharp tattoo and, following the sound, Jean spies the old Volvo cruising to a stop by the waiting-room.

"Jean-ie!" A figure waves. A familiar mound of dyed blonde hair – Sam.

Jean skids over the pavement, suitcase castors veering every which way, her face pulled into a grin.

Sam unrolls the window. "Hurry up, honey. I'm in a no-parking zone!"

A car behind honks.

Jean dashes around to the passenger side, opens the door, and tosses her suitcase into the back seat. She jumps in beside her mother, and they kiss hurriedly.

Sam guns the motor and swings the car out of the ferry terminal in a cloud of dust and exhaust.

As Jean catches her breath she watches her mother. Nothing has changed. A fast shot of relief.

Sam turns and meets her stare. "You look terrific, old thing," she says, and gives her daughter's knee a quick squeeze.

"Do I?"

"You haven't written in weeks. We were worried."

"I've been busy, but I've thought of you lots."

"Good!" Sam slaps the knee briskly. "The music must be going well for you."

Jean understands this to be a question. Instead of answering she crosses her legs and looks out the window. The car purrs along, nearly soundless on the shelf of freshly laid asphalt. A cool breeze streams into her face: air-conditioning.

They turn into a street parallel with the water. Big new houses set back from the road are surrounded by impossibly lush flowers in full bloom. Hibiscus, bougainvillea. Between buildings flash patches of glistening sea water.

"It's lovely," breathes Jean.

"Isn't it?" Her mother is pleased. "We're delighted to be out of Toronto. It was getting too big, too dirty."

21

Goodbye Bowery, the screech of sirens, the howl of drunks, the smell of spilled Thunderbird. That word again.

"I read about you in Betty Dewart's column," Jean says.

"You saw that?" Sam chuckles. "Where?"

"Colette sent it to me. What's this about a secret announcement?"

Sam's fingers slide up and down the wheel. The car responds with a tremor, and Jean keeps an eye on the broken line fast disappearing beneath them.

"It wouldn't be much of a secret if I told you."

Jean backs off. "All right, I'll wait."

Funny how there are no people on the street and it's not even dark yet. No one perching on his stoop with a beer can cheering on a ball game. No Puerto Rican kids hanging out on the corner with a ghetto blaster cranked to high decibel screech.

"Colette arrived from Toronto," says Sam.

"What? She's here already?" exclaims Jean. Her chest tightens. For some reason she assumed they'd arrive at the same moment.

"She took the red-eye last night. Do you realize this is the first time the family's been together for two and a half years?"

"How is she?"

The car cruises to a halt to let a small dog cross the street.

"Same as usual," says Sam. "Except she's taken to wearing army fatigues." The car rounds a corner. "Nelson's influence, I gather."

They travel on for a while in silence.

"And how's Dad?"

"Your father's fine," says Sam. "By the way, an old pal of yours is coming to Vancouver this weekend. A fellow New Yorker."

"Oh? Who?"

Sam continues to look straight ahead.

"A certain Mr. Takahashi."

"Yoshi?" Jean tries for a tone of normal interest. "That's certainly a coincidence." She swallows. "Does Colette know?"

"She must. There's a big ad in the morning paper. He has a new record."

"Ahhh." Jean lets the news sink in. A bee of anxiety zaps crazily around in her stomach.

"Here we are!" says Sam, rolling the tires over a long driveway of fresh gravel. "Our little *pied-à-terre*."

◻

Hooray, I'm back, Colette. I'm home!

Colette was living with her boyfriend in an apartment near the old police station. I couldn't wait to surprise her – two years. I'd changed a lot.

Weird walking through that part of Toronto, the Polish market, with its bakeries, pirogi joints, and sausages hanging in windows. She'd written me about her apartment, a third-floor walk-up next to an auto-body shop. I still couldn't imagine her with her own place, away from Dundeen Square. Did she take her dresser with her? I forgot to look. Would she still live in spartan Japanese-style simplicity? She's still Colette, I reminded myself, pushing through crowds of people on the narrow sidewalk. She'd be pleased to see me – but what if she wasn't?

The door opened to my knock, and her face spread with surprise. "Jean!" Then we hugged like I imagined we would and of course cried because it had been so long. Oh, Jean. Oh, Colette. Then we laughed at our red eyes and wet cheeks, and she pushed me into the apartment where there were walls lined with Mexican serapes and Moroccan cowbells and posters from rallies and rock concerts. A giant photo of Karl Marx hung at the top of the stairway. I guess her Japanese phase was over. She went into the kitchen to make camomile tea and told me to roll a joint, the stuff was on the table in the wooden box.

23

"Where's the man?" I looked for signs of his existence.

"He's out," she said. "At a political meeting."

"Oh."

"And what have you been doing for the last two years?"

There was so much to tell, and I began to wonder, just for a moment, if I'd be able. How could I explain going to school in Manhattan? "I sit in Washington Square, Colette, and read a book while all around people roller skate, drop flaming swords down their throats, deal dope – everything's there, things you can't imagine – and, Colette, the man I've been going with, the married professor who publishes stories in the New Yorker – it's over now. He decided to stick with his wife and it hurts, Colette, sweet glorious pain."

I sat dumbly, words lodged in my throat like dry toast. We watched each other over aromatic tea, checking out adult faces and bodies. I'd gained weight and become plumpish, rosy-cheeked. I looked over her shoulder at the bookshelf and read titles. Where would our conversation begin when there was so much?

Then something went click, a gear I'd sworn not to use, the beginning of the end of us. I said, "Do you remember the time . . . ?"

And laughing, resigned to it but a little ashamed, we dug into reminiscence, that durable cactus. Yoshi.

That's all I had to say. Then "Montreal". Our smiles broadened, overlapped.

"How did you feel when you realized we'd be staying in the room with him?"

"Terrified," I admitted. "Thrilled."

"And when the bellboy came in . . . "

" . . . and there we were sprawled on the floor on hotel mattresses. He didn't bat an eyelash."

"But he wondered, all right." A trill of shared laughter. "After all, what were we, seventeen, eighteen?"

Brief silence as each re-enacted the scene. More tea.

"What a remarkable dream it was," Colette said, dead serious.

I shook my head. "Nothing like it can happen again."

We continued the story, incident by incident, breath by shared breath, as if we were one person all those years. We remembered his house with the yellow door, the black car, the thick white rug, the jasmine tree in a pot, his *yukata* and olive skin. And, Colette, the music.

Marijuana lapsed into the Italian wine I'd brought, and Colette produced freshly baked oatmeal bread and a tub of peanut butter. She had furniture, clothes, dishes, shapes of her own. I caught a sniff of the interior of her fridge, later used her bathroom and saw his toilet things neatly stacked on the tub's edge. Scissors, toenail clippers, razor, Brut.

Our talk surged forward as if we needed to pass through each phase of our shared life just to get to this point.

We were lying on the couch, half drunk, unable to finish a story because we were laughing so hard, when he came in. His shadow crossed the rug before us, elongated by the evening light. Colette pulled herself together and made the introduction.

"Nelson," Colette waved. "I'd like you to meet my sister, Jean, who you've heard so much about."

We kissed gently, on the lips. His beard grazed my cheek. He was dark, older, long-haired, and wore a blue turtleneck and jeans. He must have heard a piece of the conversation, or felt a tone.

"Going over old times?"

He said it lightly, but I felt caught out, guilty. Colette looked once at me, then almost visibly moved her heart from us to him and said, "Maybe that's all we have now."

My own heart crumpled as if kicked. Colette, I could not bear what you said, its naked tone, the grave disloyalty. The man was there, smiling and wise.

Chapter Three

Jean steps down the precarious log stairway along the cliff face, reaching at one point for a non-existent handrail. Not built yet. She nearly hurtles into the darkness of watery cold Juan de Fuca Strait before regaining balance. She sits on a step and pauses for breath and nerve.

The sea air is almost too pungent, piercing her nostrils way back into her head.

She thinks of calling Colette's name. The dark is suddenly frightening. She has left the range of the coach lamps and the fluorescent bug-zappers mounted on poles in the garden.

She cups a hand to her mouth and cries a wolf wail — "Ow-owww" — then holds her breath and waits, her ears filling with the racket of crickets and the rhythmic slap of waves.

"Ow-owwww": the answering call from below. Again Jean lets one go, full-throated and animal proud, and slips down the remaining steps, one after the other, on her behind.

She wobbles to her feet on the final step.

A tall, slim shape is pressed flat against the shoreline, the posture so familiar Jean could sketch its silhouette without looking. She waits until she feels the sureness of sand beneath her feet and nearly speaks. But a flurry of words screams through her head like a flock of birds, knocking her off balance again. She strains at the darkness, hoping to be masked a while longer.

The shape moves toward her, soundless over sand. Suddenly Jean is wrapped in an embrace so tight that sea and sky disappear and she's a small rock surrounded by a wiry starfish. She can feel her tears wet Colette's shoulder, and her ears, blocked since the plane's descent, pop at last. A rush of clear warm sound pumps in, and she can hear the roar in her veins, a sound like the sea, only higher.

"Come and sit on my rock," says Colette.

She leads them to a stone platform, far enough from water so they won't get wet, yet near enough so the largest waves peter out inches away, leaving a clogged outline of silt and seaweed. Jean perches cross-legged, scraping her knee against the remains of an oyster.

"When did you get here?" She hugs herself, chilly now that Colette has pulled away.

"Early morning."

"You must be beat."

"I am."

The sea fills up the silence.

I saw you with him, she begins numbly. But even thinking the words causes a swell of nausea. There will be a reply and explanations, descriptions, and reasons drawn. Too clearly.

So she finds herself bone-silent again. When she leans forward something invisible presses tautly against her belly.

"Your hair looks good," she offers.

It's been cut short and sticks up straight like a hairbrush.

Colette runs her fingers through it. "You don't think it looks too butch?"

"Naaah."

They are silent, each monitoring the other's shallow breathing.

Last winter, Colette came to New York to visit. Jean had cleared the weekend and planned it start to finish — but Colette wanted to go off on her own. She'd leave the apartment dressed in something she'd just bought on West Broadway, something with wide shoulders, and not come back till early morning. She said she needed to explore on her own, find her own piece of the city. Only on the final night did they curl up on the sofa over steaming mugs of cocoa, Colette pale from lack of sleep, and talk like old times. Colette spoke of Nelson, whom she intended to marry. "What if he's the wrong guy?" she kept asking, then started to laugh. "You're supposed to *know*, Jean." No wonder she was confused, with Yoshi just left in some penthouse apartment, towel wrapped around his waist, smooth chest glistening with sweat.

Colette reaches into an inner pocket and pulls out a pack of cigarettes. "Want one?"

"No, thanks."

"Good for you."

Jean watches as Colette inhales, only the lit tip visible in the darkness. Her movements are as natural as if she needed the smoke for breathing. She looks like a young guerilla, darkly handsome like the Middle-Eastern soldiers on the six o'clock news. Does Yoshi find her exotic? Innocent?

"Did you get a chance to look at the garden?" asks Colette.

"A little. It was nearly dark when I arrived. What do you think of the house?"

"I like it," says Colette. "Hopelessly bourgeois, of course—but it's got style. It's like one of those Mobius strips: the outside's inside and the inside's outside."

Jean nods. Maybe she should smoke. It looks so intense and reflective.

"What do you make of the secret announcement?" she asks. "Dad just smiles and taps his pipe."

"I know," snorts Colette. "We're supposed to keep guessing. But I'm not that curious."

"Neither am I," says Jean quickly, then adds, "Maybe they're going to announce that after all these years they're not married and we're illegitimate—"

"And now that they're getting older they've decided to tie the knot," completes Colette. "Not bad. Dad just became a Canadian citizen."

"I didn't know that!"

"I only found out by chance. He's so damn secretive—and ashamed."

"Ashamed?"

"For capitulating after all these years."

"Why didn't I hear about this?"

"You're away."

"So are you!"

"Not so far." Colette curls one leg under the other.

Jean begins to feel a new wave of resentment. Sucked in already. That familiar sensation that they're all so fragile, a nest of thin-shelled eggs under attack.

"Have you missed me?" asks Colette suddenly. The cigarette drops to the ground.

"What a question!" Jean means to leave it at that.

But Colette's eyes remain fixed on her, daring her. Now she could say something. Colette is aching to confess, begging for it. Any simple line will do—"Have you seen 'Him' lately?"

No. Why should she make it easy?

"I always miss you," says Jean. Her tone is stiff as new skates. "I'm always looking and can't believe you're not in the next room. Isn't that silly?"

"Not silly at all." Colette looks away.

They listen to the low crash of waves. Jean's head buzzes with excitement.

"Yoshi's going to be in Vancouver," she announces. She doesn't dare look at her sister.

"That's right," says Colette carefully. "For a record signing."

"Are we going?"

"Going where?"

"To see him, of course."

"No."

"Why not?" She's pressing in now, cornering her.

Colette seems to decide. "I don't think we should dig up the past. Let it lie. We're different people now. So's he."

"Exactly why it would be interesting."

"You don't understand, do you?" accuses Colette.

"Understand what?" Jean fakes innocence.

Instead of replying Colette slips off the rock. "Let's go up to the house and make some tea. It's getting late."

Jean follows Colette's rapid tread up the rickety log stairway. It's a fast pace in the darkness, and Jean has to hurry just to keep her sister's outline firmly in sight.

"How's Nelson?" asks Jean, spooning honey into the steaming mug.

"Fine. As usual."

They are sitting in the breakfast nook. The house is quiet at last. Girdling the kitchen wall is a belt of copper pots, shining like armour. Jutting up the centre is a giant butcher block armed with knives and cleavers in descending order of size. It has taken ten minutes to locate the tea kettle.

"What's he working at these days?"

30

"He's still with the *Third World Echo*." Colette pauses and takes a sip from the mug. "They've made him editor-in-chief."

"And are you still working for them?"

"I am" — Colette puffs out her chest — "Circulation Director, Community Liaison Officer, and Production Manager of the *Third World Echo*."

"No kidding!"

"It's not a big operation," allows Colette. "Our subscription base is maybe three thousand, and we do another thou at newsstands."

"Didn't you once say they tapped your phone?" says Jean. "Have you been raided?"

"No," scoffs Colette. "We're not threatening, yet. But Nelson's got ambitions. He'd like to try controlled circulation — like *Homemaker's*."

"You've got to be joking."

"Not at all. Just because it's never been tried . . . Anyway," Colette finishes lamely, "we'll see."

"Why didn't he come?"

"What — out here?" Colette looks astonished.

"Is that so outlandish?"

"God, yes. He'd feel trapped. He married me, not the whole family."

"Sure, but — "

"We're not a couple that does everything together, if that's what you mean."

Jean didn't mean anything in particular, so she just nods. Picture of Nelson with his goatee, then later the bushy Castro beard and bandanna. Flash of Nelson (from a recent Polaroid snapped at Colette's twenty-third birthday) shaved clean with cropped hair and a dreamboat smile. Always facing directly into the camera, radiating white teeth and confidence.

"What about you?" asks Colette. She reaches her hand across the table and touches Jean's. "New York still agrees with you?"

31

"I like it there," admits Jean, pulling back. "It surprises me that simply living in a place creates a life – a home."

"Really?" Colette looks unconvinced. "Of course, you're going to school still – "

Jean takes a deep breath, sets the mug on the table, and looks her sister in the eye.

"No, I'm not. I've quit music!"

It's the first time she's spoken the words aloud. How certain they sound!

Colette starts. "What are you talking about?"

"I just couldn't do it any more." Jean cracks the table with the heel of her hand. The sound echoes in the big room. "Everything started to seem silly. A hundred grown men and women following scores as if they didn't have a thought in their heads. Audiences that don't listen then stand up at the end and demand an encore. I can't believe in it."

Colette strains backward in her chair, away from the pounding hand.

"Most of all, it's me. I've gotten so the cello makes me physically sick. If I hear it on the radio I run to turn it off. It makes me puke. It's like I've been doing the wrong thing all along, for the wrong reasons."

"What wrong reasons?"

Colette's voice is level, but her face has suddenly paled.

"Let me tell you the picture I've had in my head all these years," continues Jean urgently. "I see myself, dressed in black, walking across a stage to thunderous applause. A short bow, then – then I sink into the cello, wrap myself around it so there's nothing between me and the music – until the last note." Jean swoops her bow arm into the air, almost slugging Colette. "When suddenly I realize where I am. There's a breathless silence then – *boom*. Tremendous applause. I stand up, bow once, then glide off-stage."

Colette eyes her curiously. "What's wrong with that picture?"

"What's wrong is that I've depended on it for ten years.

It was Paradise. I thought I had it!" Jean feels herself toppling down some hill, her feet struggling to meet the incline.

"Now the whole act disgusts me! It's so self-indulgent. I used to think I was working for the higher cause. *Music.*" Jean spits out the word. "I think I was just obsessed by the glory of penitence, like those obscure orders of nuns who still sleep on beds of nails—I thought someone cared. No one cares!"

Colette stares at her sister with an expression of bewilderment. "This just doesn't sound like you. You were always so sure. I was certain you'd make it—out of blind obstinacy if nothing else."

" 'Make it,' " repeats Jean wryly. "There's nothing to 'make' any more, nowhere I want to go." She leans heavily into the chair. "The worst of it is, even though I know this new understanding is wisdom, I wish to hell I hadn't lost the original picture. I like it better. I want it back."

"Well," says Colette and pauses. She looks around the room at the posters of Switzerland, London, and China.

"Maybe you need to do something else for a while. Take a rest."

"I am," insists Jean. "And it's worse!" She stares accusingly at her sister. "It just makes me realize that I've been feeding a fat, grotesque lie."

Colette's mouth forms a cautious "O".

She's trying to figure how much I know, thinks Jean. It's killing her.

"Guess what," she says, more to herself than Colette. "Years ago, Sam said something that made me angry. It was when I announced I was going to study music in New York. She said, 'Take other courses, too. Learn about philosophy and literature and politics. Don't become a cowboy musician, with nothing but noise on your mind.' She was right." Jean pauses. "But boy is it *scary*. I feel

33

like I've been tossed off a moving boat without a life preserver."

"You know how to swim," says Colette with a slight smile. Then she makes a scraping sound with her chair.

"It's late," she says. "I'm going to bed."

"Bed?" Jean is taken aback.

"We can continue the discussion later." Colette yawns loudly. "But right now I'm dead tired."

Jean continues to stare at her.

"Do you have a watch?" asks Colette. "*Nanji des'ka?*"

Automatically, Jean pulls back her sleeve. The words come to her. "*Sanji jippun mae,*" she says, counting it out.

Colette grins triumphantly. She presses a hand against the dimmer switch until there is only the blue glow from the stove's pilot light.

Their room is at the end of the hall. Two sleeping bags are neatly spread on the floor. On each is a pillow and a toothbrush, still in its package.

They undress in the dark and slip into the bags.

"Jean?"

"Mmmm?"

"You haven't seen Yoshi in New York, have you?" The voice is carefully offhand.

Jean is alert. "Only once. Why?"

"When?"

"I'm sure I told you." Jean waits a beat. "He played at Carnegie Hall the first spring I was there."

A short silence.

"You didn't go backstage, did you?"

"No. I was with someone."

And I wouldn't go without you, Jean adds silently. She listens for further questions from the dark, but there is nothing, only the steady breathing of someone pretending to sleep.

34

□

Why didn't I go? The part about being with someone is a lie. If Colette had seen him down there on the stage half a mile away – a black-and-white dot poised over the miniature Steinway – she would understand. I applauded with the rest of the audience. It was an evening of Chopin. It was sad; I didn't know this man, there was no connection. Perhaps, if Colette had been there with me . . . I thought. Like the times we waited until the concert was over, counting off movements until the climax, which was seeing his larger-than-life figure standing outside the dressing-room, elated but tired.

Once, when he was playing the *Emperor* Concerto at a student concert, a young man no one had heard of was conducting. We sat on the hard seats of the second balcony, a dollar a shot, waiting for intermission so we could sneak down to the more expensive seats above the keyboard.

The concert seemed long, and Yoshi kept trying to hurry it up during the solo parts. When it was over we whipped backstage and beamed, "It was great, Yoshi!"

He scowled. "It was hor-rible," he said, savouring the word. "So-o boring. I couldn't believe that guy. You know we take eight minutes more than we are supposed to."

When he saw our discomfort, the scowl became a "what-can-you-do?" grin, and he guided us down the hallway with an arm slung over a shoulder of each of us. Yoshi and us.

"You have to carry me," he said, suddenly going limp. Giggling, we supported his body, all 130 pounds, out the door onto Victoria Street.

"We go and have supper," he declared, suddenly reactivated. "Is that a good idea?"

"Sure," we chorused. We didn't tell him we'd already had a full meal at home.

35

I've never been backstage at Carnegie Hall. You probably need a special pass.

Chapter Four

Jean wakes up much earlier than intended to the sound of car doors slamming. She unzips the sleeping bag part way and stares at the ceiling. Morning light glows through the slats of louvered windows, making staff-lines on the opposite wall.

She peers over at her sister, who has curled into a ball in the corner. Probably isn't used to sleeping without Nelson. A new thought occurs to her: has Colette changed her name? She has to know immediately. Still locked in the bag she caterpillars across the polished floor.

"Colette?"

A phlegmy sound is followed by a rearrangement of limbs.

"Colette!" Sharper now.

Colette's eyes flutter open. "Mmm?"

"What's your name?"

An odd expression passes over Colette's face. She rubs her eyes then draws herself up on one elbow to inspect her sister.

"I don't get it."

"Your last name. What are you using?"

"Oh." She falls back onto the pillow, closes her eyes, then says, "Same old name. Colette Hopper. Don't worry, I'm still me."

◻

The wedding, if you want to call it that, occurred last March. I got the phone call from Toronto late one night.

"I'm going to do it."

"Do what?"

A giggle. "Marry him. Next Wednesday."

I shook the sleep out of my eyes. "Hold on. Start again."

"Nelson and I have decided to get married."

"Oh." Slow comprehension. "Why?"

Another giggle. "Why not? Anyway, I'm calling to warn you."

"What do Mom and Dad think?"

"They don't exactly know yet. But it can't come as much of a surprise. We've been living together for two and a half years."

"Yes, but–" I swung my legs over the side of the bed. "You're still so young!"

"Young shmung!"

I had another thought. "You're not pregnant?"

"God, no." A nervous laugh. "I'm too young."

"What's that date again?" I gazed at the wall calendar. March was a Zen garden with raked pebbles surrounding a big rock.

"The twelfth. But I don't want you to come up."

"Why not?"

I'd never get back to sleep. There was a row on the street outside—someone ramming a bottle against a car.

"Because it's not going to be a 'wedding' wedding. We're just hopping down to City Hall for ten minutes, then we head home, back to work."

"That doesn't sound like much fun. What's the point? Aren't you going to have a party?" I began to chatter enthusiastically. "Listen—I could come up a few days before and organize something, nothing elaborate, just a few friends—"

"Thanks Jean, but en-oh. This is the way we want it, plain and simple. Private."

"Why did you even bother phoning me?"

Outside was the sound of a siren approaching. Maybe someone was being murdered. On the phone, in the background, I could hear a man declaiming in a foreign language.

"*Please*, Jean." It was a genuine plea. "It's going to be tough enough explaining to Sam and Dad. I was counting on you to understand."

I forced myself to sound cheery. "Sorry. It's just that I've been asleep, and there's a ruckus outside my window. Listen, can I at least send you guys a present? Towels? A soup tureen?"

"Nothing too bulky," advised Colette. "We've got enough junk in the apartment." She hesitated. "I'd really love you to be here—"

"So why don't I fly up!"

Colette sighed. "If you come that means Mom and Dad, and suddenly it's a family event." She paused for breath. "It's not what we want."

"Colette?"

"Yes?"

"Who's that speaking in the background?"

"Oh." Colette sounded relieved. "That's Nelson with

the Berlitz records. We're learning Spanish. There's just a teeny chance the paper might send us to Central America. Don't tell anyone. It's still up in the air."

I gripped the receiver. Central America.

"*Cuando tiene usted más apetito, al mediodía o por la noche?*" the man repeated.

"Jean?"

"I'm still here."

"I better go now. This is starting to cost."

"Goodbye – and good luck."

"Thanks."

"And give my best to Nelson."

◻

"These are favourites of your father's," declares Sam. "I don't like blue cheese at all."

"Neither do I," says Jean. She stands in the middle of the kitchen with an apron tied around her waist, hoping to be useful. She drinks coffee from a white mug with "A.M." printed in giant letters on it. The kitchen is air-conditioned, and Jean shivers. Ace, part spaniel, sleeps on his mat in the corner. She remembers the day they brought him home from the Humane Society in Toronto: a whimpering bald pup who slept for a week with a clock ticking in his basket.

Sam dumps a load of bread crumbs and parsley onto the built-in marble slab. "Here's what we have to do – are you watching?"

In answer, Jean stands close by and observes the routine. Her mother takes a spoonful of the cheese mixture into her palm and rubs her hands together in a circular motion to produce a ball. Then she rolls the ball over the breadcrumbs so they stick. When this is done she absent-mindedly pops it into her mouth.

"Oh," she grimaces. "I forgot, I don't like these."

There is a sudden awful smell. Ace stirs on his blanket and sweeps his tail back and forth.

"Ace!" Sam wrinkles her nose without looking at the animal.

Jean examines her mother's hands. They are plump, almost childlike. They dive vigorously into the cheese batter for a refill.

"Where did you get the bracelet, Sam?"

Sam stops and wipes her forehead with her upper arm.

"This thing? Your Aunt Teresa gave it to me. She made it at that course she's taking in San Miguel de Allende. What do you think?"

"It's nice. Looks sort of Aztec."

"I guess so." Sam inspects the piece. Squares of turquoise have been worked into a geometric pattern against silver. "Though I don't know how she can stand to do such finicky work. It would drive me wacko. This bracelet is her offering, since she's not coming to the party. She even sent Martin a strange pendant with a bird on it. Can you imagine?"

"I haven't seen her since she left Uncle Bob," says Jean. "Does she have a new fellow?"

"I'm sure that's the real reason she's not coming," confides Sam. "I didn't invite the chap she's living with down there, some potter. Why should I? He's no friend of mine, or Martin's." She waits for Jean to disapprove. When Jean doesn't say anything Sam asks, "Where's your sister?"

"Still asleep."

"Really? I don't know how she can with all this activity. Pour me a coffee, will you, dear?"

Jean obeys.

"Jean!"

"What?" Jean splashes hot coffee over her wrist.

Sam is pointing at her left hand. "Look how long your nails are!"

Jean's eyes follow the direction of the point. It's true. Since she stopped playing, her nails have grown to a normal length.

"Is that all?" She makes a fist.

41

Sam stares, puzzled. "Martin insists that a cellist . . . "

At that moment there is an explosion of laughter, and two men burst into the room. One is Martin. He is holding a glass of Scotch in one hand and his friend's elbow in the other.

"Look who's here, Sam!"

Sam turns pale. She wipes her hands on her apron and says slowly, "Cody Sayles. What on earth . . . ?"

Jean scrutinizes the newcomer. He's big, mid-forties at least, vaguely bohemian, and sports a full beard. His large head is shaved bald. Could be someone from the university. Plays the double bass, she guesses. Bass men are often bald.

"Hi, Sam," says Cody Sayles.

Sam reluctantly extends her hand, but Cody ignores it. Instead he reaches his big arms around her and lifts her clear off the oak floor in a bear hug.

Sam endures his grip, her mouth pinched into a tight smile.

When he lets go he steps back, grinning boyishly, and stuffs his hands into the pockets of his khakis.

"This is our daughter, Jean," says Martin. "Jeannie, meet Cody – an old friend."

"Pleased to meet you," says Cody. He crosses the room and brushes his lips against her cheek. She feels the wiry scratch of beard.

Startled, Jean laughs.

"Forgive me," says Cody. "It's just that I'm so happy to meet you. We've been out of touch a long time, your folks and I. And here you are" – he shakes his head in wonder – "a grown woman." He nods toward Sam. "She looks a lot like you did."

Sam shoots her husband a stormy look.

"We came to get Cody a beer," says Martin quickly. He pulls a can out of the fridge and snaps it open. When he passes Jean he whispers, "Your mother putting you to work?"

42

Jean nods. She tries to think of something to say, but he has turned away.

"Shall we go and sit on one of those expensive rocks in the garden?" Martin says, steering Cody out of the kitchen.

Sam crosses her arms and watches the two men exit.

When the door is shut Jean says, "Who was that?"

Sam is still eyeing the closed door, not trusting it.

"Cody Sayles," she mutters. "A very old story."

"Oh?" says Jean, waiting for more. There is no more.

Something about Cody reminds Jean of the men at Buffy's, the Seventh Avenue bar she stops in after teaching the old people. Maybe it's the boyish face sunk in a middle-aged body. Like Scott, a bearded painter in his early fifties whose skin and clothes are stained with paint and nicotine. He always wears bib overalls and a denim shirt, and his greying hair is tied back in a ponytail. "Hi, Jeannie," he waves. "Come and cheer me up."

"How's the work going?" she asks, slipping onto a neighbouring stool.

He cringes. "I said cheer me up. Jesus, Jean, I've got to get out of here." He pounds his glass on the counter till beer splashes over his wrist. "If I could get a little bread together I'd scram outta New York so fast you wouldn't see a blur – you wouldn't even smell me."

"Where would you go, Scott?" As if she doesn't know.

His jaw sets dreamily. "Connecticut, maybe, or an old farmhouse in New Hampshire. All I need is a barn, a fucking barn with a skylight so I can paint, do nothing but paint. No bar scene, no women, no nothing but goddamn snow and fields." He gulps the final ounce of beer and signals for another. Jean and the bartender exchange winks.

"Sounds good, Scott. When are you going?"

"Maybe in a year, if I get a teaching job." His voice rises to a near shout. "This place is devouring me, I can't work

43

any more, the art scene sucks. Look at SoHo." He pronounces the word with inimitable contempt, "So-Ho-Ho," then smiles, suddenly grabbing Jean around the waist. "How'd you like to come and live in an old barn in Connecticut with me, Jeannie?"

"Sure, Scott, sounds like fun."

"No more bullshit, no more landlords, no more filthy air, just nature and"—he thrusts a fist in the air—"*Art!*" He pauses then leans wearily against Jean.

"Another drink, my Canadian frien . My *warm* Canadian friend."

Sometimes she goes away then, before his hand starts to wander under her blouse. Since his face stays the same she's not sure if he realizes he's doing it. Later, when the bar starts to heat up with the younger crowd, Scott lurches home, scowling. He never asks Jean to join him.

Sometimes she stays, or heads to another bar further uptown. It's not that she drinks much. Occasionally, she'll admit to herself that she's waiting for someone. And if she meets someone else while she's waiting—that's all right, too. Yoshi won't mind.

When Colette wakens, Jean is stretched on the back deck with her feet propped on the railing. A newspaper lies beside her, held in place by a Mexican vase.

Unseen, Colette watches her sister for a while. It must be nearly noon, with the sun shot high in the sky and few shadows. Jean's eyes are open but staring ahead, unfocused.

"What are you thinking about?" says Colette, perching on the railing. She eyes, without alarm, the sheer drop of ten feet below.

Gradually, Jean swings her gaze around to her sister.

"Lots of things," she says. "Everything."

"Everything," nods Colette. She cricks her head back and squints into the sun.

"While I was helping Sam in the kitchen," continues Jean in a quiet voice, "she suggested I come out here, to Victoria, to live for a while."

"Really?"

"I told her that was a ridiculous idea." Jean sighs dramatically. "But now, looking over the cliffs, smelling the fresh wood and flowers—I'm tempted." She shades her eyes. "Quite tempted."

"What would you do here?"

"I don't know. Who cares? Maybe go back to school."

"Music?"

Jean jerks her feet off the railing, nearly upsetting her sister.

"No!"

"Take it easy."

Jean tries to. "Colette," she muses. "If you could change one thing in your life—no matter how impossible it seemed—what would it be?"

Colette stands up and turns her back to Jean and the house. She can see the ribbon of water pulled taut between sky and cliff.

"I don't think that way," she says.

"Try," urges Jean.

"I don't think that way," repeats Colette distinctly. "If something is going to change, it's because I make it happen."

"But don't you ever wish you could live scenes over again, with your present insight?"

"No." Colette whirls around. "I have no desire to live backwards."

Jean lowers her eyes.

"Why are you asking this?" says Colette.

"It's so hard," replies Jean, testing.

"What is?"

She takes the plunge. "So hard to talk to you like a normal human being. There's too much luggage—I mean baggage." She giggles nervously. "We know so much about each other."

Colette smiles. "Yet know nothing."

Jean leans forward, hands clamped over knees. "That's true. There're things I'm dying to ask you—but I don't dare."

Colette arches her eyebrows. "Really?"

"Do you believe in straight talk, even if it's painful?"

Colette stares intently at the floorboards. Under her brief brush of hair the skin reddens.

"It's more complicated . . . " she begins. "We're talking about two different people and two different minds. Sometimes it feels like you're waiting to pounce on me."

"How?" presses Jean.

"I have to defend myself . . . "

"Explain that," demands Jean.

"See?" Colette raises her head. "You're doing it right now. Not letting me be what I've become. You want me to be the person I was, that you think you remember. I can't be that for you."

She spreads her palms in apology.

Indoors, the telephone rings.

They stop and listen.

"Isn't Dad home?" says Colette.

"I think so."

Still no one answers.

"I'll get it," says Colette, and makes a run for it.

◻

Sunday mornings during one winter Yoshi rehearsed with the Hart House New Music Ensemble. They did a twentieth-century series, which he led from the piano.

We had to get up early to catch a glimpse of him those icy mornings. I hopped out of bed, 7:45 A.M., into the still house and in a jiffy broke four eggs into a frying pan. The smell yanked Colette out of bed.

46

At the dining table, placed cunningly against the window, we kept an eye on the progress across the street.

"He's opened his curtains."

"There, he just took in the paper."

Yoshi had the *New York Times* delivered to him on Sundays.

"Did you see him?" Voice high-pitched and anxious. "What was he wearing?"

We tugged on Hudson's Bay parkas and mukluks and prepared to shovel the walk. This was our self-proclaimed Sunday chore, whether there was snow or not.

"Don't look up, Colette, keep shovelling."

"I can't see anyway, my hood's too big."

Our fingers froze inside woolly mitts, and we could feel our faces crack an unbecoming red after a blast of polar wind. We worked slowly so it wouldn't be done too soon. I had a special edging technique where the shovel got pressed against newly created walls of snow. It took a long time.

At last . . .

"He's coming!" Colette sang between clenched teeth. We weren't supposed to look up right away. Our tactics involved a cool disregard followed by sudden recognition.

"Hello, Yoshi," I called finally and waved a knitted hand. A string of snot had looped itself across my mouth and I wiped, fast.

Loping down his own unshovelled walk he lifted both furry arms (for a while he sported a buffalo-hide coat) and crossed them over his head several times.

"Hello, girls. How are you?" he called, face radiating that toe-curling smile.

"Fine," we chirped, grinning furiously.

Sometimes the Thunderbird took a while to get started in the cold, and we'd listen to the motor cough and heave, half hoping it wouldn't catch.

Later, around 12:30, we positioned ourselves at the crest of the hill, a long block north, where he passed on his way back from rehearsal. At that time it was a parking lot, a flat, open prairie that got all the wind, and we stood, hands plunged deep into pockets, stamping blood into our toes, and waited for the raven flash of metal to swoop up to the stop sign. Our idea was that he would offer us a ride home and follow it up with an invitation to lunch. This never happened, but not for lack of trying.

"I hear a car, Colette!" My neck bristled.

"Don't you dare turn!"

The car stopped, spun slush onto the sidewalk and us, and gunned forward: a souped-up family ranch wagon with a child's face pressed against the rear window. Breathe again.

When we had nearly given up I felt Colette's hand on my padded elbow. "It's him, Jean. I know it!"

So fast did it occur that he would be half-way down the hill before I focused on the familiar vehicle and perhaps got a glimpse of black hair.

"Now what?"

"May as well head home." We watched as it took the curve, parting a ridge of slush, and disappeared. A moment later we strained to hear the muffled thud of a car door.

At least, we consoled ourselves, we'd gotten it right: the positioning, the time, everything we possibly could have considered. One of these days he would see us. The one thought, too awful to contemplate aloud, was that he *had* recognized us – but chose to drive on.

The bedrooms began to change. First to go were the steel beds, dragged down to the basement so the mattresses could lie flat on the floor.

Then everything had to be white. We had to earn the money ourselves, for paint, brushes, Varsol, and drop sheets. Luckily it was still winter, and we could shovel the walks of the neighbourhood. It took a month and four major snowstorms. One long weekend of round-the-clock painting and both rooms were completely white. I (Maki) did trim, while Colette (Rikko-san), being taller, managed the roller.

It looked so good when the rooms were empty we decided to leave out the furniture.

"Where will you put your clothes, your books, all your junk?" worried Sam.

"We'll find a way."

"Who do you think you are?"

Books could be arranged in a neat row on the floor against the wall, with an earthenware jar as bookend. Clothes were more difficult to hide, though we each had a small closet for hanging things. If we could just fit everything into the closets.

"You can't, there's no room."

The halls were littered with bookcases, dressers, and knick-knacks.

"We'll find a way."

We built shelves out of mandarin-orange crates to go inside the cupboards. Underwear went in one, shirts in another, and so on. Everything fit snugly in its new quarters.

The rooms started out looking nearly identical: white and spare. Then Rikko-san found a long feather; I arranged a *tokonoma* — alcove — containing a tiny vase with a single dried flower. Rikko-san pinned her kimono to the wall; I hung Japanese calligraphy prints. One day I got fed up and took everything down so my room was bare again.

"I like the emptiness," I explained.

Martin called it the Cell.

"What do you *do* up there?"

"Think. Read. Dream."

I sat in bed and pressed visions of Japan against the bare white walls; cherry blossoms and ancient twisted trees, the click, click of *geta*, and the shimmering cone of Mt. Fuji rising from a cloud of mist. Images shifted one into the other with the grace of a Noh play.

One day Martin came home with "presents" for both of us. Matching desks. Regular desks with vertical drawers and a map of Canada on top. Nothing you could saw the legs off.

"I thought you girls would be delighted," he said.

We nodded sadly.

"What the hell's wrong with you?"

"They just won't do, Father."

He refused to take the desks back to the store. Down to the basement they went, with the rest of our oversized furniture.

"Until this nutty phase of yours is over," he said.

"Tabemash'ta ka?" Have you eaten?

Rikko-san ladled the glistening snow peas onto a section of the plate, then arranged them in careful progression like fingers of a fan. The last pod she allowed to drop from six or seven inches above so it caused a very slight disruption in the pattern. A breath of wind from outside shuffled the leaves of the miniature orange tree.

The scoop of rice settled in the centre like a fist of snow. Pickled cucumbers and *daikon* – radishes – surrounded it like a necklace. *Hashi* – chopsticks – were laid carefully to the side of the plate.

She repeated the performance on a second plate and when both were assembled, nodded. She and I, clad in dark blue *yukata*, knelt at the low table, resting our buttocks on our heels. Pressing our palms together, we bowed, then, with the *hashi*, carefully picked off a grain or two of rice and placed it on the table. For Buddha.

"What are you doing?"

"I am meditating."

"What on earth for?"

"Shh, go away."

We began to practise *zazen* more or less regularly. I was more disciplined about it, setting the alarm for an unearthly 7:00 A.M. Immediately on waking, I tucked the round *zafu* pillow under my behind. I kept track each day of how long I sat and what came to pass. Always I wore the black cotton kimono for *zazen*, and after wrote something on a scroll of rice paper with a bamboo brush.

The passing of one cloud
marks the ravens.
Two abreast.

I illustrated the poem with a coarsely drawn tree: two quick strokes with the flutter of brush for branches.

It took years to become enlightened. I planned to attain *satori* by my eighteenth birthday. By then I would be through high school.

Rikko-san was less systematic. She often thought of meditating but, in the end, preferred to sleep the extra hour. After, she would be annoyed both at herself and me.

"Who do you think you are – a monk?"

I allowed a thin smile to shape my lips.

For her fifteenth birthday Rikko-san received a special gift from me, *The Book of Tea*, by Okakura Kakuzo. It became our bible.

The *chanoyu* ceremony began with the percussive twang of the *koto*. Soon a voice, sprung from the space between notes, began its nasal voyage.

Fu ki

To o

I u moo

Ku sa no o na

In the mood now, we knelt quietly at the table and examined the rock, chosen by me for its rough yet delicate form, that lay casting a slight shadow. A thin layer of moss covered one ridge like an alpine meadow. The kettle came to a boil. Rikko-san, as tea-master, rose and lifted the kettle off the burner and poured steaming water into the pot. We had been unable to find authentic *cha*, and the fragrance arose from conventional Chinese tea.

Myo ga

To o

I u moo

Ku u sa no na

The voice droned on while the *koto* sighed and clanked out an indefinite rhythm.

As Rikko-san poured into the round tea bowls her kimono sleeve drifted into the stream of hot tea and dangled there uncontrollably. She began to giggle, a soft nervous eruption. Looking up, she caught my fierce eye. "I dare you to disrupt this ceremony," my gaze said.

Rikko-san pushed the wet sleeve under her arm and finished pouring.

In a low voice I began to recite:

"The sun sets
behind Mt. Fuji.
Tea splashes into my new bowl."

And with cupped hands we brought the scalding tea to our lips.

□

Colette returns from answering the phone. She looks puzzled.

"What's up?" says Jean.

"I'm not sure." Colette presses a finger to her chin.

"Who was it?"

Colette unfolds a piece of paper and reads: "Sergeant Suknaski from the RCMP."

"What did he want?"

"Dad."

"Dad? Why?"

"I didn't ask," says Colette. "You don't."

"Did he sound . . . friendly?"

Colette considers this. "Cordial, but reserved."

"In what way?" Jean swings around.

"He wouldn't leave a message. I offered."

"Maybe it's something to do with becoming a citizen and working at the university. Maybe he has to get some security clearance," suggests Jean.

"Yeah," says Colette distantly. She refolds the paper and slips it into her pocket.

"What are you thinking?"

Colette shakes off the question. "Remind me to tell him when he gets home." She blows on her hands. "Feel like going for a walk?"

"Sure." Jean bends down to slip on her shoes. A gull drops onto the deck and pecks at something between floorboards.

◘

I found the pictures of the Zen Stone Garden in a copy of *National Geographic.*

For a long time I just stared at the cluster of photographs, one a stark image of a robed monk bending with his rake over the sand.

Groups of large and small rocks poked out of the vast expanse of perfectly combed sand – like nothing I'd ever seen before. Yet, at the same time, in some mysterious way, I recognized it.

A quick look out into our backyard was chastening. Once someone had begun a rock garden on the hill. Otherwise, the strip of land was merely trampled grass, and the only thing poking up was an ancient rusty swing set that hadn't been used in five years. Lately, the entire back-yard had been ignored in favour of a newly constructed sun deck.

I dragged Colette outside.

We emptied the old sandbox, thumped at hardened clumps of sand and dirt with the back of the shovel, and proceeded to spread the sand over the haphazard grass. We hauled the swing set into the cellar and collapsed it.

"Mom will have a fit," Colette pointed out.

We stared out at our rectangle.

"Not if she sees it when we're done!" I began to lift rocks from the crumbling rock garden and place them at intervals over the plain of sand.

"How do you know where to put them?"

"I just know," I said, with more confidence than I felt.

The scale was wrong—too small. In the pictures some of the rocks looked as tall as the monk.

"We'll think in miniature," I announced.

The day crept by.

Colette lay under a tree and sipped lemonade. Sweating, I continued to position rocks and to rake. The pictures in my pocket became wet and wrinkled from frequent con-sultation. It seemed that every time I'd finally get the blan-ket of sand combed into perfect furrows there would be some fine adjustment to be made to the rocks. Despite my delicate tip-toe through the garden, marks would be left.

"It's not smooth yet," Colette said for the tenth time.

I discovered I couldn't "fix" little areas. It always looked patchy. Long constant strokes of the rake were all that worked. One small mess meant the whole area had to be covered again.

At last.

Colette rolled to her feet and looked long and hard. Wordlessly, I handed her the clump of soggy photographs.

She smoothed them out.

"Not bad," she conceded. "In fact it's good. Very good."

At that moment we heard the car pull into the garage and the slam of car doors. There were joyous yelps of "free at last" and Ace, our crazy, floppy-eared dog bounded into the backyard. He leaped up on my leg, and before I could grab his collar made a quick skid through the stone garden, leaving a trail of scuff marks and a tell-tale dribble on the tallest rock.

Laughing, Colette handed me the rake.

Weeks went by. Every morning and every evening I tended the garden.

Standing on the sun deck with a cocktail in his hand, Martin surveyed my handiwork.

"It certainly isn't a *garden*," he observed. "It reminds me of postwar England and those depressing acres of rubble where buildings used to be."

"I think it's quite nice," said Sam. "But I like beaches."

Sometimes, for inspiration, I'd look back at those photographs of Ryōan-ji. Every time I saw that shaved-head monk in his tattered brown robe bent over the rake, I felt a surge of indescribable longing.

I tried to organize Colette into my ritual of raking.

"No, Jean. It's such a thankless task. You know it's going to get messy again."

"That's just the point!" I insisted. "It's never finished!"

One day after about a month and a long dry spell, the stone garden was at its zenith. I knew exactly how to rake in curved strokes around the rocks, forming eddies of sand.

I no longer left glaring footprints to clutter up the purity of the landscape.

I called Colette out to see.

"This is just how I want it," I exclaimed proudly. "It is perfection."

"You're becoming cocky," Colette said. "You should

know there is no such thing as perfection. Anything can happen—even this!"

Then she danced into the middle of the sand plain, threw herself down on her back, and before my horrified gaze swept in the sand, with her hands and arms, the shape of an angel.

That evening, no matter how carefully I raked I couldn't get rid of the traces of that angel. Its outline hung on, mocking my burst of vanity. I tried to remember the monk and his calm labouring, but I was mad, good and mad.

Chapter Five

It's bright out, flowers are in hectic blossom as the sun beams through a near-cloudless sky. A light wind tosses the smell of sea and pollen through the air.

"Let's take Ace, he needs the exercise," says Colette. She whistles and slaps her thigh. "C'mon boy!"

Ace stirs in his basket, lifts his ear flaps, and rises.

"Let's go, Ace," urges Jean.

The dog grunts indulgently and follows them down the steps, his gait a dignified shuffle.

"What's wrong with him?" asks Jean. "Does he have a bad leg?"

"No one around here walks him. He's seizing up."

The trio crosses the pebbly driveway toward the freshly paved sidewalk. Dog prints are stamped into the concrete.

"There's Dad—and Cody Sayles," points Colette. "Shall I give him the phone message?"

"Later, when he's alone."

Colette nods. "You're right."

The two men sit on webbed deck chairs under a recently planted sapling, which provides scant shade. A Scotch bottle tips precariously on the grass nearby.

Jean begins to sprint, shouting encouragement. "Come on, Ace. Show them how fast we can run!" She's a teenager again, and Ace a near-pup full of the devil.

Ace bravely bounds alongside a few paces before slowing to a trot, his tongue hanging out.

"Careful!" warns Martin.

Jean skids to a stop. "Of what?"

"Ace isn't young any more. He's arthritic in his hind end."

"Oh?" Jean stares at the familiar pet, who whinnies happily, thumping his tail on the ground. It's the same goofy, sad-eyed face, just a trifle grey around the muzzle, the eyes perhaps less clear.

"Poor old dog." She tousles the curly hair on his head. "It didn't occur to me that you weren't just being lazy." She turns to Colette. "He doesn't *look* old."

"I would go with you," yawns Cody, shifting heavily in the fragile chair, "but I'm too comfortable." He tilts a beer can to his lips.

The neighbouring house is a hundred yards east. It sprawls low to the ground like a bunker and is covered with rough cedar siding. An air-conditioner is wedged in a front window and whirrs loudly. To the side a hole is being dug for a swimming pool. A big black cat prowls the circumference of the hole, tipping in bits of stone and dirt. At first, Ace displays no interest, even when the cat arches its back and coils its tail into a fiddlehead.

"Look, Ace—a *cat*," encourages Jean. She smacks her hands together.

Ace ambles over to the pit, keeping well away from the hissing cat. He trots around the rim, skidding on bits of rubble.

"He's not seeing too well," says Colette.

There is a surprised yelp and Ace suddenly disappears.

The two sisters dash over the freshly upended dirt just in time to see Ace skidding down the wall of the pit, his forepaws frantically scratching at the mud.

"Ace!" shrieks Jean.

She leans helplessly, meeting those panicked dog-eyes as he slowly slithers downward, etching a ten-foot waterfall into the clay wall. Reaching bottom he tumbles an awkward somersault, then huddles whimpering, fur caked in mud.

"What are we going to do?"

"He's probably all right – just scared," determines Colette. "Ace!" she calls.

He gives a plaintive yap.

"I feel terrible." Jean covers her face. "It's my fault, I encouraged him."

Colette gives her a sharp jab in the ribs. "Lend me a hand. I'm going down."

"How?"

"Same way he did."

Colette rolls up the cuffs of her paratrooper suit and kicks her shoes onto the ground. Crouching, she begins to slide down the pit on her rear, leaving in her wake a streak of smoothed dirt.

"What are you going to do now?" shouts Jean.

Colette reaches Ace with a soft bump and starts scratching his neck and chattering into his ear.

"Coming up," she calls after a short while. She gives Ace a hefty slap on the behind and, with a startled yelp, he lunges toward the wall of the pit, scratching his way up a good four feet before sliding back. Directly behind is Colette, digging one foot after the other into the soft clay, butting the animal with her head.

59

Jean lies on her belly at the side of the hole and waits. Within moments she is able to grab Ace's collar and heave him up the last couple of feet. Then she does the same for Colette, yanking her hand in hand.

"There. He's fine," says Colette, slapping the mud off her pants. "I just thought of something: Ace in the hole." She laughs then eyes her sister. "I'd hate to have you around in a *real* crisis."

Irritated, Jean leads the way back to the road.

They continue the walk in silence. Colette hangs back a few yards, followed by an unconcerned Ace who gives little yips of pleasure at his rescue.

◻

There's a sound fingernails make when scraping for dear life. It freezes me, I can't help it. I don't know what to do. The sound etches right into my brain, numbing it. Once I had the job of handing Dad tools as he shingled the garage roof. It was a blistering hot day, and I squinted into the sun, tossing up nails, hammer, and shingles as required.

"Pass another pack," he yelled. The perspiration squeezed off his face and onto his bare chest. He was slippery as a newborn. Bored and a little mad at spending my Saturday roasting in the sun, I reached for the shingles and hurled the pack toward his outstretched hand.

My aim was lousy.

He lunged for it – too hard – then started to slip. Just like Ace, except he uttered no sound at all. There was nothing but the ungodly scrape of his fingernails raking into the fresh shingles, pulling tar and asphalt away in a little shower.

I stood and watched, feet rooted to soil as he skidded, first slowly, then faster, but never fast, in a slow-motion dive to the forsythia bush below, a dive that gave me all the time in the world to act. But I didn't.

I must have yelled. Sam dashed out of the house, eyes wide as hubcaps. She gave me one sharp accusing look before turning to her husband who was moaning on the grass.

He was all right. He just had the wind knocked out of him. Sam helped him into the house while I tagged on behind, sniffling and dragging my feet. As he sank into the chair, face white as plaster, he smiled wanly and gave my shoulder a little punch.

"Sorry to scare you, old thing," he said.

□

"Let's go this way."

Colette points to a concession road branching right, away from the ocean.

"Where does it go?" Jean feels tired suddenly, her feet still hinged to the ground.

The road looks bleak, leading nowhere.

"There's an old folks' home at the end," says Colette. "Or maybe it's a mental hospital."

"There is a difference."

"I know, but I forget. Which is it, Ace?"

In reply, Ace scratches himself behind the ear – a contortion that makes him grunt.

"Still pretty spry, aren't you?" says Colette, nudging him gently with her toe. "Not ready for the Home yet."

They tramp down the road, which seems endless, and Jean gets the feeling the landscape is spinning out in all directions like a sheet of silk slung from a giant bolt. No nose can store the perfumes that radiate from every blade of grass, each inch of soil, each particle of living organism.

A sign appears on the left: "ARBUTUS LODGE."

"Could be either one, old folks or schizophrenics," speculates Colette. "Non-committal, if you'll pardon the pun."

"If it is old people," says Jean, "I'd be interested in paying a visit."

"You would?" Colette looks surprised.

"In New York that's what I do, work with old people."

"Oh, that's right. I'd forgotten. But you can't just walk in without knowing someone. And what about Ace?"

"You two can wait outside."

"Maybe there will be nothing there, just the sign. Maybe they haven't got around to building it yet, what with all the cutbacks."

"Mmmm," grunts Jean, unimpressed. She knows Colette is afraid. Everyone is at first.

At the beginning she tried to pretend there was no difference between herself and them. Carefully she avoided obvious references to age. One day Mrs. Kahn took her aside before class and said, "You're afraid of us, aren't you? We're so old. Ancient. And Jews, too." The cane seemed to bend under her weight. "But remember, we can't suck your youth away; we're not . . . vampires!" She grinned, displaying her remaining teeth. "Maybe we don't want to. It's been long enough on this earth already."

Then Jean took her place in front of the microphone and flipped through her stack of notes – all twenty pages.

"So, Professor Hopper; what are you going to teach us today?"

"We're going to discuss *A Doll's House*, by Ibsen . . ." she began. The microphone screeched.

"Ach, *Nora*" someone cried in recognition.

They all knew about Nora.

"She had to leave her husband; he treats her like *dirt*, like a *child*," insisted Mrs. Schwarz, rising to her feet with the aid of a walker.

"He doesn't see she is a *person*, a woman," interrupted Mrs. Rubenstein, who had had one leg amputated after being shoved into the path of a subway. "My husband, when he was alive, he expected me every night to have dinner on the table at six, the house perfect, and the children clean and out of his way. Like that: one, two, three. Maybe I should have left him – but it is too late . . . he's dead now fifteen years."

The big room buzzed with excitement.

"He thinks he is king!"

"The husbands are the children!"

"Nora must leave him before he destroys her!"

So much for the feminism Jean had hoped, discreetly, to introduce. They'd sprinted past, leaving her blinking with wonder on the starting line.

Half-way into her second lecture she pronounced "shtetl" wrong, leaving out the second "t". There was an instant chorus of correction, which left her speechless for a moment. But they weren't angry, only amused.

"You are so *young*, Professor Hopper." They gathered after class and touched her hair. "You have your whole life."

Someone placed a dry hand on her upper arm as if to test muscle tone. They love it when she jogs uptown and arrives in sweatsuit and sneakers, cheeks rosy from the cold.

"But you should be careful: this area has gone to the dogs."

"Drugs."

"And dirty. I never go out any more."

"Lucky thing you can *run*."

"That must be it."

Ahead, blocking the end of the road, is a big modern building with a closed-in porch.

"I don't see a soul," says Jean.

"They've got the sprinklers on. Shall we head back?"

"A little further."

Jean breathes in the lushly perfumed air from a bank of flowers that surrounds the building. She imagines cars full of family arriving each Sunday, parents trying to tone down their children's exuberance, and leaving an hour later, depressed, and jammed full of lukewarm tea and soggy digestives.

"Want to sit down?" says Colette.

"Where?" The grass is wet.

"Here's a bench. I think it's where they wait for the bus."

Ace curls up beneath, grateful for the shade. Above is the hum of a small aircraft, dipping low to a nearby field. Jean feels something wet on her exposed ankle. She jerks before realizing it's only Ace's rumpled tongue. He laps the dust off her skin.

Inside the lodge a bell sounds: bong, bonggg, like a monk signalling afternoon prayers.

Still there is no one in sight, except for a man in work clothes pushing a wheelbarrow full of dirt. He dumps the load by the flowerbed and heads back behind the building.

"Do you really like living in New York by yourself?" Colette asks suddenly.

Jean twitches. "I love it," she says.

"Really?" Colette's tone is sceptical. "You know what I was thinking?" she continues.

"What?"

"I was imagining what it would be like if you moved back to Toronto. It's improved a lot since the old days."

For an instant the fantasy materializes: she could live near Colette, in a real neighbourhood with children and trees and backyards. They would meet for afternoon tea and talk for hours. And at night it would be snug and quiet, just the faint yapping of dogs and a far-off radio tuned to CBC-FM.

"Everyone wants me to come back," muses Jean. "Mom

and Dad want me in Victoria and you want me in Toronto. It's very flattering."

"Maybe it's because we're frightened for you down there."

"Frightened of what?"

"Oh, you know." Colette waves a hand. "We hear things . . . . Sometimes I picture you in some alleyway, tossed out of a moving car. Or in Chinatown, trapped in a basement opium den." She adds with a forced smile, "Then where would I be?"

Where indeed? thinks Jean. And are you afraid I'll see you with him down there and snatch the secret out of your surprised hands? Kick it across the room? I could tell your husband. Begin with that. Nelson and I could become confidants, meeting in out-of-the-way cafés for whispered confessions.

There's a rumble of tires on the road. A bus? Jean stands up, shades her eyes, and looks toward the approaching vehicle.

A snappy red sports car skids to a stop with a hail of pebbles and dust and parks nearby, away from the sprinklers. A youngish man steps out, wearing a T-shirt and tan slacks and carrying a briefcase.

"Excuse me," calls Jean.

He turns. "Yes?"

"What is Arbutus Lodge? An old people's home?"

He stares at her. "No." Then adds in clipped tones. "It's a cosmetic-surgery clinic."

He darts toward the side entrance of the lodge, pressing the thin case under his arm.

"I really like it here," enthused Mrs. Schwarz, stopping Jean in the hallway. "So much to do and no worries at all. We are treated very well."

Colette lights a cigarette and tosses the match on the ground.

They are on the way back. She hunches her shoulders to protect the cigarette from the afternoon sea breeze. Jean steps on the smouldering match thinking of forest fires. Ace lopes alongside, his nose grazing the ground. He's favouring a hind leg, curling it under like a grasshopper.

"Are you going to grow old with Nelson?" says Jean.

Colette smiles. 'I guess so. Do I have a choice?"

"Only to do it alone or with someone. I don't want anyone up close, hearing me grunt when I stoop to tie my shoelaces."

"I'm looking forward to it," insists Colette. "Besides, Nelson keeps me on the move. I don't think that changes."

"What do you mean?"

"Think of Sam and Dad, always edgy together. That's how I am with him."

"Really?" Jean is unconvinced.

Colette pulls out a fresh cigarette and knocks it against her palm. She only smokes them half-way these days, because of the tar.

Jean spies a flash of sparkling ocean. It surprises her how close they are to the edge of the continent.

"We have almost nothing in common," continues Colette. "When we *do* come together" – she slaps her hands – "bang!"

"Oh." Jean nods several times.

Of course, what did she expect? That they share a bed merely to save space? That they live together because a bottle of wine divides neatly in two?

"Back then, I needed someone strong enough to push aside that funny world we'd built. Pure Disney." Colette tosses her head back and blows smoke rings.

Jean digs her hand into Ace's furry back and rakes through the matted hair. He still likes it; he rubs against her legs and makes a noise like a cat purring.

"Nelson was strong enough, and still is."

"I see."

"If anything, *too* strong."

"Oh?"

But Colette is finished. The house is in sight and two empty chairs perch on the front lawn.

The first time Jean saw her friend Reuben was in a copy of *Art News*. She was flipping through and caught sight of this gaunt face staring aggressively into the camera. He was wearing torn jeans and a T-shirt with the sleeves rolled up. She thought he looked like Bruce Springsteen. A week later when she met him at an opening she told him that. He laughed and seemed pleased. His red paintings lined the walls of the shoebox-sized gallery, and it was like being caught inside an artery. She was surprised at how frail he looked in real life, stalking up and down, nervous as a kite, with his hands stuck into the back pockets of his jeans.

They have an understanding. Right now Jean can't remember exactly what it is.

"What does he mean to you now?"

"Nelson?" Colette glances at her.

"No, Yoshi." Jean delivers the name like a delicate piece of china.

"I don't know," confesses Colette. "Sometimes I think it would be better if it had never happened."

"But it did," insists Jean.

Colette looks at her sadly. "You're still full of him, aren't you?"

Jean catches her tongue on her teeth. Not now. Not yet.

□

We used to phone him, just to hear the sound of his voice, then pretended to have the wrong number.

"*Moshi moshi,*" he'd answer.

We hung up, then practised saying it — "*Moshi moshi*"

—till we got it just right. We started answering the phone that way ourselves. Martin got upset. He thought it sounded silly.

"Like a Chinese greasy spoon," he said.

One day Colette noticed he'd left his car lights on. His battery would run down. It was a serious matter. Any decent neighbour would let him know.

We climbed the concrete stairs to the little house with the yellow door, our hearts leaping. We would save him from certain disaster.

Yoshi didn't answer our knock for a long time. When the door finally opened a crack we could see only his round face, bleary eyes, and shock of black hair.

"Hello," he said sleepily, once he'd registered who it was. "You wait here. I get dressed." Through the crack we saw him fly up the stairs in his robe.

"Rats," Colette said. "We woke him up."

We waited no more than thirty seconds before he returned and opened the door while buttoning the front of his brown corduroys. He'd pulled a ratty sweater over his head making the hair go into even more of a shock.

"Come on in," he said.

We started to state our mission, but he wasn't interested. Instead we slipped out of our shoes and sank into the thick carpet. We were through the door, on the other side. The song began in my head.

"You want tea?" he called from the kitchen.

"Sure—please," we answered, and followed him into the little room.

The kitchen was clean and uncluttered, with none of the endless jars and boxes that littered each surface at home. A sumi brush painting of a Japanese maple hung on the white wall.

"You try dry fish?" He held out a cellophane packet full of shredded material. I reached in, picked out a piece of thready substance, and dropped it in my mouth. Salty. My lips puckered around it as it stayed chewy, like gum.

"In Japan kids eat this for snack," Yoshi said, watching my reaction.

Colette took a much smaller piece and chewed daintily.

When he turned to pour hot water into the pot I mentally gauged his size next to mine. I was taller already – no denying it. But, though slender, he had a wiry body, and he probably weighed more than me. For some reason this was comforting. I noticed no outline of underwear under his trousers and realized in his rush to get dressed he hadn't bothered. He was naked underneath. Always naked underneath. For the first time I felt a different kind of stir, almost a sigh of the whole body.

When I turned to Colette, her eyes glowed and she flagged a hand to her forehead in a mock swoon.

Later that night she came into my room and said tentatively, "Would you sleep with him if he asked you?"

Horrified, I said, "Of course not! What a ridiculous idea."

Colette sneaked away. I went back to my scrapbook of photos and clippings, pasting in a radio program with his name in it.

I looked at his feet: small and perfectly formed. He'd slipped into a pair of *zōri*, the thong dividing the slender big toe from the others. Exquisite doll feet. As we waited for the kettle to boil he asked, seemingly out of the blue, "What is most embarrassing thing that ever happen to you?"

This took some thought. There had been so many.

Was it the time he'd reached over and touched my hair saying (with a knowing smile), "Why do you look at me so curiously?"

But Colette piped up, without shyness, "Last year during a swimming meet at school I dived in for the three-hundred metre relay, and the top of my suit came off!" She hooted with laughter. I cringed with embarrassment.

He looked at her seriously and said, "So what did you do?"

"I don't remember."

He didn't stop looking at her, waiting, I think, for the rest of the story. It was as if he didn't get the point of it.

"What about Jean?" he asked finally. His gaze focused bright, daring me.

But I told a harmless anecdote, calculated to cost little dignity. He laughed and said, "Now I tell about my embarrassing time."

"What happened?" we asked eagerly.

"Two weeks ago" – he lifted two fingers in the air – "I go to give concert in Cleveland, Ohio."

"Cleveland," we nodded.

"And we rehearse on Tuesday Beethoven Two – you know that music?" He hummed a few bars, slightly off-key.

"Conductor is very good man, but so-o-o stern." He pulled a dour Germanic face. "And maybe I am nervous or something. What happens – this is so bad I can't believe it – on concert night, which is Wednesday, I have in my mind Beethoven Three – that is famous one everyone knows, eh?"

He hummed a few bars, waving an imaginary baton.

"So when conductor gives downbeat I see right away my mistake, but I think it is *his* mistake." Yoshi grabbed his own head and shook it violently. "So I make this loud noise . . . "

"What noise?" we encouraged.

He opened his mouth wide and made a rasping sound, like a rattlesnake.

"It is so loud," he giggled, "and hall is so quiet, because this is very big conductor, and everyone looks at me. Conductor has sharp eyes, like schoolmaster. I feel so terrible I nearly fall into floor and, you know, next day in paper critic says, 'Japanese Pianist Afraid of Beethoven'."

"That's awful!" we screamed with glee.

"Oh, well." He shrugged. "That's the way it goes."

He poured tea from the pot into little clay cups with no handles. We flinched from the heat but held on.

"You want to hear some piano?" he asked.

"Oh, yes!" We exchanged delighted glances.

We trooped after him, holding our hot cups, to the studio at the back of the house. Along the way I peered at a gallery of photographs on the wall – all famous musicians: Bernstein, Ozawa, Solti, Ashkenazy – with pen-marks scrawled across their surfaces.

"For Yoshi, with warmest hugs and kisses – Lenny."

"With respect and affection, G. Solti."

The picture of Ozawa was autographed with a flurry of Japanese calligraphy.

When I stopped to read a long message from Yehudi Menuhin, Yoshi glanced up.

"These are nice people," he said. "We give each other music, then a picture to remember. They all look so – what's that word?" He scratched his head in a parody of thinking. "Dignified. You should see what they get from me; this crazy guy playing piano backwards!"

I never figured out what he meant by that. He must've got a word mixed up; but he often did that – used an expression in an odd way. For a while people he liked were called "straightguy", all one word, regardless of sex.

The studio was a little room crowded by the grand piano and a stack of music. One wall contained a sliding glass door that looked out into a scruffy garden. Yoshi had no time for weeding.

So this was where the work happened. We stepped carefully, reverently, through the bits of tossed score, teacups, and even a set of barbells on the floor.

"I guess you think I need bigger room," he said, noting our quick once-over. "But I like this; is so personal."

He sat on the piano bench, and we hovered over his shoulder. Yoshi Takahashi was about to play a private

71

concert for us! The vision swung in of his diminutive figure in tails strolling on stage, bowing, flipping the tails behind before sitting, making two quick adjustments to the stool, wiping the sweat off his palms. A nod to the conductor, the raised baton, the deep breath, the hands poised above the glistening keyboard . . .

Yoshi twisted half around, straddling the bench, and dipsy-doed through a few chords with his right hand.

"What do you like to hear?"

"Anything!"

He looked thoughtful, then sucked in an exaggerated breath. Raising his shoulders to his ears he let his hands plunge onto the keyboard, *bam*, into the opening chords of Beethoven's Fifth Symphony.

Bam-bam-bam-*baam*.

What was this? Another suck of breath and he stood up, clenching his teeth like Lon Chaney.

Bam-bam-bam-*baam*.

Then he reached down and picked the steaming teacup off the floor and took a sip. The pedal was still held so that the last chord resonated noisily in the little room.

We giggled quietly, still not sure.

Suddenly he spun around, wiped his forehead, and said, "I think that is enough of serious music — is *so* much work to play Beethoven." He made his face sag onto the keyboard for a moment.

"I bet you know this song!" Suddenly his fingers moved easily over the keys, tooting a speeded-up version of "Tijuana Taxi", humming the horn line alongside.

We tapped our toes shyly and watched the fingerdance, now so easy and loose, and the narrow slope of his shoulders as he bopped from side to side. His left hand rolled a few embellishments, sometimes shaking the beat around, causing a brief but definite kick. The piano tap danced as he passed the ball about at will, behind his back, over his head, twirling on the little finger like a Harlem Globe-trotter.

"Wooah!" He slowed down, twisting his right wrist, making the chord break into an arpeggio. Then, a pause.

"So!" His hands sprang into the air and he stood up. "Now I have to finish my nap."

At the door we paused, slipping into our shoes as he waited, hands in pockets, yawning.

"See you soon," he said.

We waved, said goodbye, and trotted down the steps past the still-lit car, chattering.

"I thought he looked tired; his eyes had bags under them."

"He was kidding with the Beethoven, right?"

"Do you really think he was glad to see us, or just pretending?"

"Yoshi never pretends anything."

And something else had taken hold. I sat with my cello and began picking out the tune, trying to imitate that sure-footed dance. But on this side of the yellow door the music was strained; an invisible metronome clocked out the relentless beat, hour by hour. Yet I knew if I practised long and hard enough, one day I would be able to join him, a fellow dancer on the world's stages. It was the only way.

Chapter Six

"Hello?" Jean peeks into the sunroom. It is bright green — the effect of sun bouncing off green floral wallpaper. At first she sees only the big man, Cody. He is hunched on the window seat, one leg drawn up to his chin.

"Hello," comes the reply. Following the voice she steps into the room and sees her father in the corner. He is in a familiar posture, bent over the eighteenth-century German-made cello, rubbing a chamois over its soundboard.

He twirls the instrument on its endpin so he can rub the back. She feels a faint ache of longing.

"Come on in," says Martin. "I thought I'd flex a little for Cody. Don't feel obliged to listen."

"I'd like to," Jean says and pulls up one of the wicker

chairs. There's a bright green cushion on its seat that matches the wallpaper. "I haven't heard you play in a long time."

Martin laughs. "I don't expect my family to join the ranks of devoted fans. Cody, pass me that little red box on the window seat. It's resin."

Cody tosses it without changing position.

"Do you play anything?" he asks Jean.

"Oh, I play some cello," she says quickly, not looking at her father.

"More than some," says Martin. He eyes Jean. "At first I thought she'd never be more than so-so, until suddenly she got the bug, went at it like a house on fire . . . "

"Please . . . " says Jean.

"She's got a nice bow arm," says Martin. He finishes resining, then demonstrates with a fluid movement across the strings. "See that?" He flops his elbow up and down. "A good, loose elbow, not like so many of my students: when the going gets tough their bow arms stiffen into boomerangs. Say, Jean, want to give it a go?" He pushes the cello away from his body.

She waves him off. "I'm not in the mood."

"I'd like to hear you," says Cody.

"I'm here to listen," she says firmly. "It's Dad's turn."

"Artistic temperament?" Martin raises his eyebrows.

"So? Are you surprised?" This comes out as a whine, not coolly sardonic as she intended.

Her father leans into a series of double stops, digging into the strings so they vibrate full out. With his head tilted toward the soundboard he says, "Just disappointed."

Cody is watching, wondering why she's upset. But she can't help it. In fact, she stares down at her stomach and coughs a few times, to calm down.

"I'll play you a crowd pleaser," her father says. "Fauré's *Élégie*. You like this one, Jeanie, eh?"

He begins to play the corny warhorse that sings through

her heart every time; it's so "cello", the instrument born to it. And peering up she sees her father hunched over, his head now balding, bobbing up and down so his chin nearly knocks the top of the instrument. He hugs it and at the same time digs in as if to probe the unheard sounds.

Cody is leaning, head against the window, eyes half shut. The room tightens, squeezing vibrations out of the furniture and window panes. The overtones jumble up in her ears, singing a queer harmonic accompaniment to the Fauré.

This is the same cello he let her play during a recital back in high school. She was in a quintet with a viola that played passionately out of tune. The program was long, and the quintet was at the end of it. After, Martin had come backstage and soberly shaken the hands of all five, as if they hadn't just sawn their way through the fragile branch of Schubert's *Trout*, fourth movement only (thank God).

Then there was the first time she'd seen, really seen, his "playing face". It was a century ago, she couldn't have been more than six or seven. She had just wandered in, lonely one Sunday afternoon, to watch him practise. As she crouched on the floor, cross-legged, she realized he hadn't noticed her entrance. His eyes were squeezed shut so tight his lashes disappeared. With each sweep of his bow his mouth tensed into a grimace. This face belonged to whom? And where was he, so far from her? She ran out of the studio to her room where she dived into bed, clutching her pillow. Years later when she told him about this, he seemed disturbed. She'd only meant it to be funny.

"Wait, Jean!"

A hand curls over her shoulder and she stops in midstride. She turns but doesn't say anything.

Cody lets his hand drop. "Are you all right? I thought you looked sick in there."

He blocks the light from the window.

"I'm fine."

Her toes chatter inside her shoes. He won't keep his eyes off her, one hand propped against the wall near her head. He's even dressed like a hunter: L.L. Bean from his boots to the expensive chamois shirt. She drops her gaze. Yes, there it is, the leather pouch holding the top-of-the-line Swiss knife.

"Excuse me." She darts under his arm and heads toward the back door. *Bang.* Her face slaps against the polished glass. She lets out a gasp of surprise and pain.

"That you, Colette?"

The call comes from Sam in the next room, where she is greeting recent arrivals. "Why don't you join us in here?"

"I have to do something," calls Jean, rubbing her injured nose. She slides the door open and steps out onto the cedar deck. It has been freshly urethaned and feels sticky underfoot. She jogs down the steps, one, two, three, heads down the little pathway fringed with sculpted bushes, takes a shortcut over the man-made stream with its little eddies, and on to the edge of the garden where it has been allowed to grow wilder. By some oversight the grass hasn't been mowed. A mid-afternoon breeze off the ocean dusts her face with sawdust and pollen. She finds the top of the stairs and looks down the cliff to the beach below. The water is stirred up since last night. She steps briskly down the log stairs, confident in daylight. Before stepping onto the beach she removes her shoes, then lands one bare sole after the other on the welcoming sand. It cups her feet and sifts between her toes. That must be the rock she and Colette sat on last night: there's a little pyramid of ash and cigarette ends scattered over its surface. And there are the two sets of footprints, now indistinguishable after a day's wind. She picks up a handful of flat stones and shoots one out at an oncoming wave. It disappears with a plop. She bends over sideways, works her wrist back and forth a few times (remember the relaxed bow arm!) and gives a sidearm pitch into the surf. It skips over the waves beautifully, like a gull.

If only she could do it herself; if only the water weren't so damn cold. She picks up a length of kelp, crazy giant licorice, and tosses it about like a lion tamer warming up. With the final whip she lets it sail into the ocean, where it floats for a few moments, then disappears.

◻

The tide was out, and the clay shone with snails. This wasn't Georgian Bay where we usually summered, but some beach in Nova Scotia where we spent a rainy July one year. Father was Musician in Residence at Acadia.

I fumbled the giant beach ball and watched as it swept into the air and began a quick skim over the clay toward the ocean half a mile out. Without thinking, I ran after it.

Imagine me, a speck from shore in a red bathing suit slipping through the wet clay toward the speck of ball, which grew smaller in its sail to the horizon. I ran past the cement breakwater, wind pushing from behind like a big hand. Underfoot the pellet shells of snails scraped my skin, but I kept my eyes on the striped ball. If I blinked it would disappear. Near water the clay got even softer, and I started sinking to the ankles. Finally I couldn't run and instead kicked out each step, thrashing mud over my white legs where it clung in thick drips.

From shore came sounds. Colette, calling in fear – "Come back!" – as she lost sight of the ball. Later she said I was no bigger than a dime.

The ball disappeared, possibly on its way to Spain – even Africa. One blink, one pause, and I'd lost it. Stopping with a messy slide I looked about – acres of wet clay – then toward shore where Colette stood, a tiny flutter of motion against the rocks. "How did I get here?" Sudden terror. I was completely alone. Any minute the tide, the dangerous, fast-moving wave we'd been warned of, could sweep in and dash me against the cliffs.

78

"Colette!" I semaphored, arms wild.

She danced up and down.

I could hardly walk, snails and clay squishing between my toes, so I stepped into my previous footsteps, surprised at how far apart they were. The wind tried to push me back out to sea like an undertow.

At last I got back. Colette was wide-eyed and furious with fear as I fell exhausted on a rock. How close it had been. If I hadn't heard her and stopped, I would have chased that ball, chased it clean into the Atlantic Ocean.

◻

A gull swoops to pick off a fish swimming carelessly near the surface. A dozen other gulls chase the first, and the fish is swapped around and torn at until there's nothing left.

Jean practises wading in and standing till her feet and calves get so cold she can't feel them. Then she stays a little longer, just to see what that's like. She looks through the clear water and stares at her toes, then at the surrounding pebbles. They always look better when they're wet; it brings the colours out. Later on when you've put the rocks on a window ledge to dry they turn dull and grey.

She tosses a handful of gleaming stones at a gull, knowing she'll miss by a mile.

◻

I was practising my cello, something by Bach and tricky as hell, and as usual had the window open so Yoshi could hear if he went out. In my mind was the sound of du Pré. This was always the case: I heard someone else, the remembered music, when I was playing.

As I sank into the instrument, strapping the bow across, picking my way up the fingerboard with my left hand, Father came in. He listened. I shook my hair dramatically and plunged into an absurd and totally unnecessary umpteenth-position double stop.

"Wait a minute, Jean," he said gently. He sat down on the leather footstool, and I stopped and looked at him. As usual he was wearing a tweed suit and white shirt. He crossed his legs and rested his chin in his hand.

"Yes, what?" I asked, annoyed to have my discourse interrupted.

"Jean," he coughed awkwardly. "You are a bright girl . . ."

I beamed, let the bow dangle at my side.

"But –" He looked me straight in the eye, and suddenly I went pale, feeling something terrible was about to happen.

"You have some real talent," he said. "But so do lots of people."

While my face fell two storeys he kept talking.

"I don't want to discourage you – far from it. But keep your ambitions realistic. Music should be enjoyed by everyone, and there's no reason on earth why you shouldn't continue to play cello till the day you die, and play very competently. *But* we mustn't fool ourselves."

His legs uncrossed then realigned on the opposite axis.

"You are not Zara Nelsova and never will be. You simply haven't got the ear. Some of that can be learned" – he smiled sadly – "but only so much."

He stood up, walked over to me, and placed a hand over my slumped shoulders.

"I have great faith in you," he said. "But I don't want to see you get hurt. The world –" He paused. "The world is out there for you."

He left the room and closed the door. I remained in my cello crouch for a moment, feeling the rage curl through my system, limb by limb. After a few minutes I stood up, let the cello drop against the chair, and went over to the open window. A clear, scent-filled spring breeze ballooned my clothing. Yoshi's car had gone. I hadn't heard the door close or the motor start. Perhaps it was true: I really didn't have an ear. I closed the window. Then I played non-stop for an hour, grafting calluses onto my calluses, never letting the sound die for a second.

Chapter Seven

"Where is everyone?"

The stereo is thumping out the beginning of Berlioz's "March to the Scaffold".

"Gone to graveyards, everyone," sings Sam. She is writing things on a yellow pad. "Cody has taken the guests to the hotel for dinner so we could have some time to ourselves."

The doorbell chimes.

Colette hops up – "That'll be the pizza" – and returns a moment later carrying two large flat boxes.

"There just isn't time for everything," moans Sam. "It's madness, sheer madness. Jean, take a pen and write things down. No, don't! Get some paper plates from the kitchen and – are you listening? – napkins, first drawer on the left . . .

She's not listening, you know. In a moment she'll call out—"

"Where're the napkins again?"

"See?" Sam repeats her directions.

"I presume that I'll carve?" Martin opens a box with the tip of a knife. "Samantha, dear, a wedge?"

"Yes. My stomach is in turmoil, but I must eat. Jean, wine on the sideboard."

There is a silent bit on the record before the smash of the guillotine. Everyone jumps.

"That always scares hell out of me."

"Are these anchovies? What am I supposed to be writing down?"

"Number one: red napkins are for the head table, white for the others. Number two: I want the students to start gathering guests at four o'clock because it will take half an hour to seat them all. And number three"—Sam holds up a finger—"you girls are to sit on either side of your father and me. And I've put Uncle Charlie beside you, Jean, and Aunt Ruth to Colette's left. I know they're dull as dishwater, but a few drinks will help. Once"—she looks briefly sad—"my brother Charlie was a comer. Quarterback of the football team and a great ladies' man."

"Uncle Charlie?" the sisters chorus.

"I know, you'd hardly believe he's only two years older than I am."

"Charlie?" Martin looks up from the slice of pizza that drapes over his hand like molten steel. "He's senile."

"Shhh." Sam slaps his wrist. "They could arrive any minute."

"Everyone wants wine? How about these plastic cups, can I use them?"

"Yes. Now, Colette, see that group of cartons over there?"

"Yes."

"They're presents, housewarming gifts. If you would bring them out one by one, I'll make a check mark beside the appropriate name on the guest list and mark in what they've sent. Everyone is to get a nice note, promptly. Maybe you girls could help me with that."

"Here's something odd-shaped. Can I open it?"

"Martin, I think *you* should unwrap, and Colette can mark things down."

"You want me to open all these? I'm trying to eat."

A pained look. "Please co-operate. What have we here?"

"Looks like a corkscrew."

"Don't say it like that, Martin, it's a lovely corkscrew."

"It's a corkscrew!" repeats Martin with enthusiasm.

"Who's it from? Dave and Marion. Look on the bottom; I bet you a dollar it's a Georg Jensen."

"Bingo."

"Got that, Colette? You're dripping sauce on the list. Why is it I feel like it's dress rehearsal and I'm surrounded by a cast who doesn't know its lines? Next present."

"There's one goddamn box inside the other. Some puzzle . . . it smells . . . ah, glass."

(Chorus) "Ahhh."

"It's broken? What a shame. Make sure you get all the pieces and put them back in the box. What was it? A carafe? Look at the box. A vase? What a shame. Why does it smell funny?"

"It's the wrapping – perfumed."

"Why don't you try that giant box from the Hilsops? They have their own antique shop, you know, since Larry retired." Sam grabs Colette's forearm. "I nearly forgot. I'll treat you girls to a hairdresser in the morning. My Antonio is very good, not old-fashioned at all."

Colette runs sticky fingers through her hair. "I just had mine cut."

"It's a clock, a wall clock and a barometer, all in one."

"Oohh."

"Where does it wind up? Must be on the bottom. Someone change the record and pour wine. Number four, before I forget, don't let your father hear this, Jean, but I don't want that man, Cody, in my sight. Make sure that Martin hasn't switched his place card. He should be at the southwest table with the gang from the university. They all love to talk, and I'm sure he'll be right at home. Number five? Number five. Oh dear, what is number five? Ah, the flag, we must put the flag up above the table."

"You're not serious," groans Martin.

"Of course I am."

"I refuse to sit under some *arriviste* symbol, Samantha."

"Number *six*. What's in that box? A shell. Why would someone give us a shell?"

Fifteen or twenty tables were set up with cloths and cutlery. The usual blast of fluorescent lighting had been softened. The lecture hall was transformed into a ballroom. Jean arrived early as the old people were filing in wearing antique evening dresses, the hems scraping the floor.

It was graduation day; not just for Jean's class but also for the course on Social Issues Today. That teacher, Professor Gloria Kroetch, sat with her small group on one side of the room.

"This way, Professor Hopper."

Mrs. Menninger, Supervisor of Programming, escorted her to a table near the front. Jean sat down, grateful she'd been warned the occasion was dressy. Under the table she curled her stockinged ankles around each other. She heard her name called and waved. Her students were all over, glowing in their freshly coiffed hair, necklaces, and old-fashioned gowns. Wheelchairs were decorated with flowers, and hands fingered printed programs.

If I can only keep from crying.

Instead, Jean smiled and smiled harder till her mouth cracked up to her ears, and still it wasn't wide enough. It couldn't be.

The ceremony began. In front was the head table manned by representatives from City College, the Mayor's office, the Home – and there was Dr. Schulman, her one male student, resplendent in suit, red silk tie, and gleaming cuff-links. He sat nervously, shifting a sheet of foolscap.

First there were opening remarks, which Jean barely heard. Then the speeches from the mayor's office and the college about the tradition of university extension in the community – blah, blah. She stared at the tablecloth and played with her fork until Dr. Schulman rose to his feet and began speaking in heavily accented English.

"We are so proud to be here today at this graduation ceremony. First I would like to thank, from all of us, our teacher, Professor Jean Hopper, who has been so interesting . . . "

He continued, praising her meagre scholarship until she blushed a furious red. Everyone in the room beamed at her, watching each twitch of her face.

The smile stayed glued on, barely.

Then the representatives from City College began to call out names of students, and one by one they walked, wheeled, or pushed walkers up to the front podium to claim their diplomas. On the way back, clutching the roll of paper, they stopped at Jean's table and grasped her hand.

"This is my first university degree!" Their eyes shone with pride and disbelief.

"Professor Hopper, I hope you know what this means."

The old Russian woman driven off the shtetl sixty years ago wasn't able to say a word. She just stood in front of Jean holding the diploma and shaking it in the air. Her whole face quivered with pride – and amazement. She was ninety-two and illiterate.

Jean couldn't speak. She hardly dared open her mouth feeling, as she did, that everything was just barely being held back.

"The girls are going to see Yoshi," declares Sam.

There is a brief pause.

"We are?" says Jean.

"Well, aren't you?"

"Don't be surprised if he's old and grey," says Martin.

How old? She has to count on her fingers. Forty, anyway. He's a Pisces, but Orientals don't show their years. Like light from the stars, their age arrives a long time after the fact.

His eyes emerald green still, or clouded by too many years in the limelight?

"He may have completely forgotten about us," suggests Jean.

"He may," says Colette, but they look at each other, mirroring disbelief.

"He may flee," says Martin, opening a screw-top of local wine. "And I can't say I'd blame him. You girls haunted him like" – he twists the lid – "like a bad knee. For a time I thought you'd come home one day bearing slant-eyed babies in your bellies."

"Martin . . . " Sam warns.

"Little slant-eyed babies," repeats Martin.

Jean, her face clamped in a smile, toys with the silver-plated corkscrew.

The old fool.

"Remember our word?" whispers Colette behind a cupped palm.

"Sure do."

Martin was "Zen-o-phobic". He wouldn't even eat Chinese food.

"How would we explain that to Uncle Charlie and Aunt Ruth?"

"Stop drinking, Martin," says Sam calmly. "Your worst qualities are displayed." She adds over her shoulder to her daughters. "Ignore him."

"Let's picture the scene, folks." Martin waves the bottle in the air. "Colette and Jean, our lovely daughters, enter breathless, records in hand, and elbow their way through the throng of admirers. 'Mr. Takahashi, remember us?'" Martin affects a high-pitched voice.

"Dad . . . "

"Hold on, I'm enjoying this. So. His eyes light up in horror and he half rises, then tips back the chair in a dead faint!"

Colette fingers her glass. "Don't mock him. If you mock him you're mocking us."

Martin pulls out a handkerchief and pretends to blow his nose. He is about to speak again but thinks better of it. Instead he gulps his wine and leaves the room.

"Your poor old dad," says Sam. She lifts the final, cold slice of pizza from the box and licks her fingers.

"Why poor?" demands Colette.

"Because he's jealous. He thinks you care more about seeing Yoshi than him."

"That's absurd!" says Jean.

Sam shrugs. "Let's clean up in here and move into the other room. *Martin!* He's hiding with the rest of the wine." She reaches out for the arms of her daughters and propels them through the doorway. "*Avanti, avanti!*"

"Did you give Dad the message from Sergeant Preston?" whispers Jean.

"Suknaski. Yes, I did. He just smiled mysteriously and folded it into his trouser pocket."

"Aha!"

"What does that mean?"

"Just . . . aha!"

The living room has a "conversation pit", a giant thumb-print in the floor lined with broadloom and silk-covered pillows. A glass-and-chrome coffee table rises up from the middle. Sitting on it is a book laminated with birchbark. The cover has been etched with a Haida motif.

Martin lounges in a corner of the oval shape. In his flannels and sports jacket he looks like a professor of history venturing into student Pub Night. He reclines with enforced ease, one hand pressed against his chin, the other settled over his thigh. He is still as slim as he ever was.

Jean sits in a half lotus, her left foot snapped against her right calf.

"Our family is certainly normal," says Colette, the words slightly slurred. They have been drinking since five. "We have no mad relative snared in the closet, and what's a reunion without the poor dreamy daughter unlocked from the asylum, circulating among guests in her hospital smock, reciting Ophelia's speech?"

"You sound disappointed," observes Martin. He is tempted to recite the appropriate lines, but isn't sure he remembers them just now.

"I am," says Colette. "We are blisteringly ordinary. We can't even ramble the overgrown trails of childhood here." She sinks her toes into the thick pile of rug. "This house has nothing of *us* in it. We're orphans."

"Orphans?" says Jean.

"House orphans. They've extinguished it all. Poof!"

"Wait a minute," protests Sam. "What about the photographs in the hallway?" She looks genuinely concerned. "I had them specially mounted for this occasion."

Colette dismisses this with a wave. "The whole field's been plowed over, toys and all. Not to be found again for centuries. Remember when you and Father decided never to fly together so if something happened to the plane we wouldn't be left alone? Well, you've done it in another way. All I smell around here is fresh cedar and new paint."

"Don't say that!" cries Sam. "You're making me feel terrible. You don't really feel that way."

"I think it's a relief," ventures Jean. "I'm proud that you've gone ahead and lived your lives without us."

"Oh dear, that's worse," says Sam.

Colette sways back and forth. "It's as if the dead came back a year after their passing only to find that the beloved survivors have cast off their mourning clothes for jaunty new sportswear."

"It's been considerably more than a year," remarks Martin.

89

Sam is sitting almost still, jiggling her bracelet.

Jean picks at the carpet, gathering its fluff into a ball. They bruise like peaches, crack like overworked clay.

Martin has shut his eyes and is humming along with the music.

Sam reaches for the birchbark book on the coffee table. "I nearly forgot," she says. "You girls haven't signed the guest book." She opens it to the first double spread, which is already laced with the scrawls of visitors. She passes it to her eldest daughter, who, after a grimace, picks up the pen.

"Good," breathes Jean. For a moment she thought Colette might dash it to the ground.

"He'll have hair growing out of his nostrils," warns Martin, his eyes fluttering open. "He'll have aged with the rest of us."

Colette's hand hovers above the page. Then she carefully draws Japanese pictographs for "Colette Hopper".

□

My bedroom was high on the third floor facing the street – and his house. Colette's was downstairs at the back facing only trees and alleyway, but she never complained. I had a clipboard to which I fixed several sheets of graph paper and so began the Chart. Like a detective I noted everything, in no-nonsense factual form.

DATE	DRESS	ACTIVITIES
Dec. 20/ 68	Buffalo coat, corduroys (brown), carrying briefcase & bag of groceries from Loblaws.	Paused to clear windshield of snow, took packets inside, left front door open, came out w/out coat and sprinkled salt on steps, didn't look up.

I took care not to be seen. To this end I devised a periscope using paper towel rolls and mirrors, but it never worked right, and I ended up crouching so only the top part of my head would show. This way I figured, if he looked up, he'd have no way of knowing it was me.

"Yoshi's gone out and I've missed him!" I'd cry.

Once, as I was passing the window I glanced out as always and the black Thunderbird was driving up. Combat-trained, I dropped quickly to the floor then raised myself slowly so my eyes flattened against the glass. He stepped out of the car, reached behind and slammed the door, then suddenly twisted so he was facing into my window, his gaze shining a direct path into mine. For five tortured seconds neither of us blinked. I was hooked into him like a minnow on a grappling hook. I fell back onto the rug.

He couldn't have seen me, I persuaded myself. He had simply had a sudden thought and was gazing distractedly into space . . . and I seized my chart, which dangled from a string, and dutifully made the day's notation.

For five years he was in every daydream as we strolled to the detested high school, kicking through leaves and slush and freshly fallen snow, with little to say so early in the morning. I saw myself on stage with him, taking the place of an ailing virtuoso – anything was possible. We whipped through some duo sonata – unrehearsed, and I played as if the cello were singing its last song, my bow spearing the air like a samurai warrior. We held our breath until the last note when, sweat pouring off his smooth forehead, he stood up to embrace me . . .

I *was* going to join his world, breathe the same thin air of collaboration.

Then one day:

DATE	DRESS	ACTIVITIES
Sept. 8/69	Suede jacket & black leather pants, carrying small plastic bag from drugstore.	Accompanied by 30-ish woman, brown hair, tweed coat. She walks ahead of him to door & waits as he unlocks it. He touches her waist & they enter. After a while curtains pulled in upstairs bedroom.

This news I yelped through the house, not ready to believe the obvious – "Colette, come and look!" – until Father said in exasperation, "Give the man a little privacy," which showed how little he understood.

We timed the visit: forty-five minutes.

"That's not long enough," Colette said.

But we weren't sure; we had no way of knowing.

Once we were taking the garbage out, three overloaded plastic bags bursting at the seams, when we paused, panting at the curb edge.

"Our family throws out more than it consumes," said Colette. She wiped hair away from her forehead.

We were glancing, as usual, across the street. His one small bag, knotted and only half full, teetered in the wind. Suddenly it began to skid gently along his patch of sidewalk, bouncing over the cracks like a ball of tumbleweed.

"Maybe we should . . ." I began.

At that moment a pickup truck with a propped-up rear end zipped through our field of vision, and we heard a faint but distinct "pop".

When the truck disappeared it left in its wake the exploded contents of the little bag. Bits of paper, crumpled envelopes, and a soup tin tossed into the air then coasted by us. We didn't have to move an inch.

Colette bent over and said, "I bet he didn't mean to throw *this* away." She picked up a stainless-steel coffee spoon.

Then I spied the mystery object. As it skimmed by I trapped it with my toe.

"What's this, Colette?"

"I don't know – open it."

"He must have thrown it out by accident, too. See, it's never been touched. There's a bunch of empty packets alongside."

"Hurry up, let's see."

(Together) "Oh, my!"

"There's only one thing this can be," I said.

We giggled uneasily, let the wet thing stretch out like a balloon. Then we checked to make sure no one was looking.

"Wouldn't it be awful if he drove up right now!"

"I'd die."

We took the thing inside and went to the bathroom to fill it up with water.

"It's huge! No one's that big!" We felt slight panic. Then suddenly I was tired and annoyed and wanted to pretend the whole thing had never happened.

"Empty it out. This is sick."

I couldn't stand to look at it any more. It wasn't Yoshi's, couldn't be.

Colette poured out the water and jammed the balloon back in its little pocket. Now what? We didn't want to get rid of it entirely; it was part of the archives now. And where would it be safe to toss such a thing?

It was decided that since I owned a small strongbox we would keep it there.

It stayed there for some months under a stash of winter clothing in the cupboard. I never forgot it was there; I avoided the area. After a while I got nervous: what if Sam became curious and hitched open the box? It would be easy enough.

I had to get it out of my closet, pronto.

We chose a drizzling midsummer afternoon when no one was on the streets. He was, as usual, away. The Thunderbird moulted in his driveway, a thin edge of rust rimming its underside. I unlocked the box, picked up the by now despised object, wrapped it in a piece of toilet paper, and slipped it into my jeans' pocket. We had the spot picked out—a sewer grill on the corner. Kneeling down I pushed the thing between the grates and heard the little "plop" as it landed in rain water. Forever gone. I sighed with relief.

Chapter Eight

I couldn't help giggling: he was trying to slip his signature ring over my finger but it wouldn't go. My finger grew white from the strain, sausagelike, but he didn't dare smile. This made it worse. Finally I couldn't hold it back any longer and burst out laughing. Then Kiyo laughed, too, and we rolled on the grass.

Colette peeked up from her place in Taki's arms. I was supposed to be necking so what was the big joke?

"I'll tell you later," I mouthed. "Every detail."

After the ring episode, Kiyo and I leaned together under a tree and he pressed his groin against my thigh. Colette and Taki lay nearby on the manicured grass by the statue; someone had painted the horse's balls red. The man I was pressed against was a near stranger.

I was a little jealous of Colette's relationship. Taki spoke English, and they had real conversations – not just about sex, either. Kiyo's English wasn't too good. But – I crowed happily – I have his ring! Maybe he really thought of me as his girl. If I squinted my eyes he looked just like Yoshi, especially the hair.

Kiyo smiled and patted my hand. He guided it under his shirt to the flat of his belly.

He was alone here, far from home, and I was his only friend apart from Taki. Maybe he loved me, and the ring was a proposal of marriage. Instantly my feelings leapt three squares. I was in love with Kiyo Yamada. He would take me back to Osaka with him and we would live in a house with rice paper *shōji* screens and *tatami* mats. He would wear a *yukata*, and I would wear a glorious silk kimono printed with flying cranes and fresh-cut cherry blossoms.

After we'd made out for a couple of hours we all stopped for a root beer and donut at the A & W, then Taki drove us home. He parked his old Ford around the corner so we could have a long kiss goodbye. My skin was feeling baked from the sun, and I'd just as soon have gone inside, but I waited. I kept an eye on the two in the front seat and heard the sound of cloth rubbing against cloth followed by Taki's short quick breath. For a moment I was shocked and lonely, until I felt the welcome hand of Kiyo twisting me toward his lips.

◻

"Remember the Dana girls?" giggles Jean. She tugs at the joint and exhales loudly. Two tokes, that's all she allows herself.

The three of them, Cody, Colette, and herself are lying on an open sleeping bag on the beach. Above are a grinning sliver of moon and a spread of twinkling stars.

"They used to escape from their boarding-school dorms

96

each night. They'd knot sheets and drop to the ground below – off to solve another crime."

"Except," sighs Colette, "there's no crime to solve. How empty life has turned out to be."

Cody laughs and tips the jug of cheap local wine to his lips. How can he drink so much? Jean wonders. An empty bottle lies in the sand next to them.

She passes the joint to her sister, then leans back heavily, breathing in the pungent sea air. For a moment her head reels; had she smoked more than she intended?

◘

We ordered Kiyo up one Christmas from the International Student Centre. There was only supposed to be one student. Our family would demonstrate a typical Canadian Christmas.

On December twenty-fifth we set an extra place at the Scandinavian pine table and waited.

"What if he doesn't eat turkey?" Colette said, looking dubiously at the enormous bird browning in the oven. One end was sewn up with big black stitches.

"Or potato," I added. "Not to mention squash, peas, and mince pie."

"Maybe we better not give him too much," Colette suggested, and we planned a sparse white plate adorned with three slivers of turkey, half a potato, and a scoop of squash.

Promptly at 6:00 P.M. the doorbell rang, and we raced to answer it, neither of us wanting the other to grab a first impression. Our heels skittered over the polished tile.

Four young Oriental men in suits stood politely smiling on the doormat, their shoulders dusted with snow. As one they bowed and bid us good evening.

We stood paralysed. Four? Luckily Sam came to the rescue in her billowing caftan. "Hello, hello!" she cried, flinging the inside door open. "Come on in. Right this way."

Humbly the six of us followed in her wake.

As Sam seated them in the living-room before a glowing fire, we received hissed instructions. "Set three more places – pronto." We dashed into the kitchen for extra cutlery, where Colette whispered rapturously, "I don't *believe* it," eyes glowing like meteorites, and I shot back, "This must be heaven!" A brief nervous hug before we grabbed handfuls of knives, forks, and linen napkins.

It was determined that Kiyo was the one who had actually been invited. He introduced himself and handed Sam a neatly wrapped gift. Taki, Endo, and Yukio were his friends from the university, no other explanation or apology.

Sam unwrapped the parcel to reveal a delicately embroidered towel "Made in Osaka", as Kiyo pointed out. Sam spread it over a radiator where it stayed for years, until they moved west.

Immediately I had spied Kiyo as the "handsomest" (most like Yoshi) and sat next to him, practising my Japanese. Everything I said made him laugh – politely, of course. His suit and tie were old-fashioned, and he bobbed his head after every remark.

"Particle-physics," he explained, was his field, same as the others. Except Endo, a tiny man in modish Beatles jacket and pointed boots who was studying "Western-style theatre."

Supper occurred without incident. They didn't seem alarmed by the food and ate with gusto, especially Yukio, a stocky, silent man, too shy to talk.

As we shuffled our bloated selves back into the living-room to continue the polite conversation, Endo suddenly declared, "Now I sing for you."

He stood in the doorway, hands clasped behind his back. I flashed a glance to Colette, then Father. He stared unblinking ahead. He had hardly eaten a thing, which was usual; he preferred to look on.

Endo's arms spread out from his side and pushed skyward, straining under an invisible weight. A surprisingly strong baritone issued from his compact body.

"I'm dre-eaming of a whi-i-te Christ-mas," he crooned, in an astonishing Bing Crosby imitation. "Just like the one I used to kno-ow."

His brow knitted, the arms dropped to his sides, and he sucked in a chestful of air.

"Where the tree are glistening–"

I peeked around the room. His friends beamed at me. Colette stared directly at the singer.

"I'm dre-eaming of a white Christ-mas–" He held the tone several beats in an edgy vibrato.

"Just–" A hand carved out a stair.

"Like–" Another stair.

"The one–" And another.

"To . . . know!" The palm had reached as high as it could go on the final note.

We applauded vigorously, then Sam poured coffee into demitasses, spiking them liberally with Tia Maria. As I passed the cups around, Colette trailed with a bowl of nuts and figs.

"Thank you." Kiyo smiled and balanced the cup on his knees as he reached for a walnut. Colette fingered me in the ribs and I knew why; for a moment, when he smiled, he looked *exactly* like Him.

◘

Some teenagers whizz by in a power boat, their laughter swelling above the roar of waves and motor. Suddenly they swerve into a jack-knife turn and nearly get swamped. There are loud shrieks as the boat rights itself and bounces over its own wake into the darkness.

"Seems like everyone's partying tonight," says Cody. He leans against the rock so his shirt tugs across his belly, threatening to pop a button. The voice is a low drawl, half drunk, half American, a stretched sound that nicks the edges off consonants.

He lies between them, breathing heavily through his mouth. At night he must snore. It was hard for him to climb down the stairs to the beach, and he grumbled all the way, even though it was his idea.

Cody rolls another joint, using his kneecap as platform. His feet are anchored by heavy hiking boots.

"Of course I'm a drunk," he says, in response to no uttered question. "If you lived in my rent-controlled dive nestled under the Williamsburg Bridge you'd hide your face in a bottle, too."

"New York?" Jean's interest is pricked. "I live in New York."

"Do you?" He stares at her, focusing slowly. His eyes have a protective shield of wetness. "Impossible!"

"Why?" Colette peers over his belly hump.

"Because she's too pure, too much of a white lass. Look at her." He points at her with his chin as if that said it all. "She's having her adventure in the big city like all the girls who come to ooh and aah at the broken-down old men and the 'artistes'. I suppose you're an 'artiste'?"

"I don't know what I am," Jean answers.

In the distance there's the tweak of a red lighthouse beacon.

"What are you doing here?" asks Colette abruptly.

With effort Cody adjusts his position against the rock.

"Why—your daddy, of course. Haven't seen him and the lovely Samantha for years. Not since the old days. Also"—he sighs—"I love to fish in Canada. I *live* to fish in any body of water we haven't managed to kill dead. All year I dream of escape; it keeps me going during eternal subway journeys to some godforsaken borough. See this gear?" He slaps his shirt and trousers. "These are my party clothes. I send away for them every paycheck, from the catalogue. They fit." He pulls the waistband of the khakis and snaps it back.

"You're not so fat," protests Jean. More bearlike, she decides, then giggles.

"Ha! Your laughter, my love, is better than trout. Drink some more wine!"

Jean sinks her head into a hollow place in the rock. It nuzzles into her neck like the chrome sink at Nicky's Hair Cuts on Eighth Street. Colette has sprawled in half sleep on the bag; she's made a little pillow of sand under the flap. Above the cliff it's dead quiet except for a radio faintly tuned to the news.

"If you hate it so much in New York why don't you leave?" asks Jean. She collects answers to this question.

"Because . . . " Cody tries to speak, then takes a quick swig to clear his mind. "Because I must earn a living. Because I'm virtually unemployable anywhere else. New York puts up with me because she has to; she's entangled me in her catacombs." There is a short silence. "Catacombs," he repeats thickly, and runs a hand over his smooth scalp.

"How did you and Father meet?"

"You don't know?" He looks surprised. "To begin with"—he leans close so she can see his beard articulate into individual whiskers—"we were buddies in New York in the fifties, back in the bad old bohemian days when the word still meant something."

"Dad?" Colette chuckles from the other side. "A beat?"

"Sort of," answers Cody. "British style. He hung out in the Village with the rest of us. Smoked pot."

"Get on!" The notion dismays yet delights Jean. "He's never talked about his beatnik days in the Village. Who would have known?"

"There's one photograph," recalls Colette. "Taken when he was about ten, with his brother. He's wearing a blazer and short pants and a private-school beanie. In the background is a big brick house covered with ivy."

101

"A fine man," nods Cody. "A passionate man."

"Passionate!" the sisters chorus, then laugh.

"You have to tell us more," begs Colette.

"Ask him, not me," says Cody, retreating. "Keep your image, what the hell, it's worked this far. I shouldn't have opened my big yap." He redistributes himself so he's lying flat on his back staring at the sky. The wine bottle, capped, rolls away then lodges in the sand.

"Martin always had music," says Cody after a while. "All I had was dumb idealism. Know what I am?" He doesn't wait for a guess. "A failed scholar. A so-called medievalist with a degree from a lean-to college in southern Idaho. You can see their ads in the back of *Time* magazine." Cody draws in the air.

"EARN A DEGREE IN TEN MONTHS OR LESS. NO EXAMS. NO ESSAYS."

He laughs noisily, a throat full of cigarettes and wine. "So I waltzed out to Idaho and shot pool for the better part of a year. And now I teach at every bogus institution that'll have me, from Jersey to Staten Island—any joint that swallows my lies. But your daddy wouldn't settle for that. He married a stylish dame and put his nose into that bloody instrument and learned it. I admire him. Wish it was a *horn*, but I admire him none the less. A fine man—did I say that? I love him. His daughters, too." He reaches over and gives them each a hug. "I can hardly believe in you; it's almost too much."

"You married, Cody?" asks Colette, her voice muffled in his forearm.

"Once," he says cheerfully. "About five years ago. It lasted three months; she was too smart to stay. Listen, having me is like swimming the Channel with rocks in your trunks. Who needs it?"

"Don't be so self-deprecating," chides Jean. "You just want us to love you. Oldest strategy in the world."

"Ouch!"

"It's true."

"Sure it's true." He coughs hard, raising his knees. "But you're not supposed to catch on so fast."

They lie still, and before long his breathing transforms to noisy snores, torn in the middle by a rasping suck for air.

◻

Yoshi was leaving Toronto for good.

Dressed in our up-to-the-minute miniskirts and poor-boy sweaters we knocked on the yellow fairy door with the excuse of saying goodbye. He took a long time answering.

"I bet he's napping," Colette said, and knocked louder. I wiped my eyes, forgetting about the coating of mascara.

At last the door opened a crack, and a sleepy unshaven face peered through the aperture. Did he always sleep during the day? It was becoming an unhappy joke. "We've woken him up," I moaned silently. "He'll shoo us away; what an ending."

But as always, Yoshi didn't let us down, and wrapping his grey *yukata* more securely he greeted us in Japanese, "*Konnichi wa*," and flung open the door.

"You've been sleeping," I apologized.

"Yes," he admitted. "But that's okay—you girls come in and talk to me. I'm going away soon—did you hear?"

"Yes, we know."

We entered the house of enchantments with its low lacquered table, the bush of jasmine, the white rug, and no chairs. We lowered ourselves cross-legged on pillows, our short skirts riding high. He sat down, too, folding his hands and tilting his head toward us.

"So. How are you?"

We were fine.

"You look very good." A frank, approving gaze. "You like something to drink?"

Flattered, we said yes. He disappeared into the kitchen and came back holding a tray with three brandy snifters and a bottle of cognac. We'd never tasted cognac before and told him so.

"I think you will like it," he said with mock seriousness, then carefully measured out three huge portions.

At first we sipped prudently, getting used to the sensation in stages.

"You girls smoke marijuana?" he asked after a while.

Colette looked at me and I looked back. We weren't sure what he wanted us to be in this case: worldly or innocent.

"Sometimes," I said safely. "What about you?"

"One time I smoke," he said. "But I don't know . . . maybe is not so good, makes you lose memory or not sleep. Are you sure?"

"Sure about what?"

His face tilted, showing concern. There were a few grey hairs poking up from the thatch of black.

"You could get sick," he said.

We laughed. We were sixties kids; we knew all about dope.

"What's so funny?" He jiggled our crossed knees. "Why you laughing at me? Do I say something stupid, make joke?"

"You sound like our parents," I said.

"I *do*?" He was shocked. "That is bad. Maybe I should mind my own business, so. What else is new?" He leaned back, his expression changing. "What happens in your school? You have dance? Rock-and-roll group?"

"We don't like dances much," Colette said with disdain. "Boys our own age . . . " She let it drop.

"And you're a lousy dancer," I pointed out.

"So who's talking, you dance like a boy." She did a cruel imitation of those boys who play air guitar, their eyes closed as they pound out a riff on an invisible fretboard.

104

I squirmed.

Yoshi roared with laughter. "You dance like this?"

I grunted something. He stopped laughing and looked at each of us.

"You are my good friends," he said, and then put one palm against Colette's temple and one against mine and slowly bonked our heads together. Gently, but we got the point.

He poured us a second drink, this time not so big.

"When I was your age in Japan," he said, "I go to a private school and have to wear this ridiculous —" he mimed a stiff collar and tie.

"Uniform."

"Uni-form. Right. Teachers are very strict, we always have to stand up and bow, we are never rude or make bad jokes to them, and every day when I come home I practise so hard on piano, three hours before supper."

"Three hours!"

"And that is not including," he emphasized, "piano before breakfast, too, sometimes hour, sometimes more. It is very hard. I never get to know anyone but family and music teacher."

"I wouldn't like that," Colette said, wrinkling her nose. "Except it paid off; now you have a good life."

This was a question.

"Sure I have good life," he admitted. "But still I have to wear uniform when I play. And, you know, I miss something. I see you girls and I feel that."

Our eyes met and for a moment I understood.

"You have lots of friends," I said.

"Lots of people," he agreed. "But is so complicated. Everyone I know is with music, and because sometimes I am in newspaper or television people think they know me. There is no one in Canada that is really close friend, like brother. I never have close friend like that, like you have."

Then he opened a package of Japanese crackers coated in seaweed and spread them on the table. We munched happily. They were brown and green and shiny, as if lacquered. Hardly like food at all. He stretched his legs out ahead of him and shook out the kinks. He yawned loudly, and we watched every move. Was he aware of our attentiveness? I believe so. The room, all beige and black, began to glow as dusk fell. An exotic smell made me think of faraway places; sounds of traffic were muffled and could be cartwheels jiggling over a dirt road.

As I was soaking into mild drunkenness he suddenly said, "I have a new record someone gives me; you want me to play?"

"Sure," we chorused.

While he was doing this Colette reached over and pressed my elbow. I squeezed back, harder than I intended.

Janis Joplin started in on "Piece of My Heart."

"I just love this," Yoshi said. "It is so strong." He reached for the right English words. "It makes me think of big moments, strong moments—you know?"

Yes, we knew. I held my breath and felt the room shimmer. The cognac had taken hold, and all three of us fell back into the luxuriant softness of pillows and furry carpet.

"So, you girls have boyfriends now?"

"Sort of," we admitted. Of course they didn't mean much, just something to pass the time, to fit in.

"What do you do with these boys? You kiss?"

He gave us a look of open curiosity. And no wonder: each time he saw us we had grown a little older, and he was the one we shared the new knowledge with. This time it was the makeup—a result of twenty minutes locked in the bathroom with Sam's equipment.

"Sure we kiss," Colette said boldly.

I looked over at her. Something had happened. Her cheeks were flushed, but her eyes had a completely open, unguarded expression. Must be the liquor, I thought, and wondered what might happen. What *could* happen.

"Remember the first time I see you girls—you were so young!" Suddenly he reached forward and wrapped his arms around us, pushing us into his chest for a bear hug. "I will miss you."

"We'll miss you, too, Yoshi." If only I'd dared say more: I love you, Yoshi. We were so close to him, buried next to his skin with only the light cloth of the *yukata*, which smelt of jasmine and sweat. We hugged him back.

"Have you seen my bedroom?" he asked, when the hug was over and we were back lounging on our pillows. The question sounded so innocent—like "Have you seen my garden?"—and we shook our heads, no, though Colette eyed me and winked. Could he be suggesting . . .? It was unthinkable.

"I show you." He slapped his hands against his knees, coinciding with the end of the song, and rose to his feet. Naturally we followed, Colette grabbing my elbow as we tottered up the stairs to the second floor. If this was what drinking did I wanted to be drunk forever.

The bedroom consisted of a large mattress on the floor surrounded by little piles of clothes and sheet music. A small upright piano stood in one corner, covered in more music. The bed, to my surprise, was neatly made. I didn't know men knew how to make beds.

Immediately he spread himself on the mattress and beckoned us to join him. We didn't hesitate an instant; none of the usual rules applied. Colette lay on one side and I on the other so all three of us stared at the ceiling. Across the street our father was watching a soccer game on TV. Sam was cooking supper. My feet, if they were to float two hundred yards due east, would land on my own bed.

The Joplin record started to play over again, and I was half listening to that, wanting to remember how it felt, so I could recreate it in daydreams. Something was being discussed, a plan I could hardly keep track of it seemed so unbelievable. We could go with him to Montreal; no, we would meet him there on Friday in time for his farewell concert. We lay, heads tucked under his arms, feeling the length of his body next to our own. He wasn't any longer than I was.

"It will be very sad time for me in Montreal. Is my last concert in Canada for a long time. I think I like you girls to be with me."

We would all stay at the Hotel Champlain. He would have the train tickets put aside, and we would get there in time for rehearsal if we wished.

After a while he went to sleep (from where we'd pulled him), and we slipped out, barely able to walk straight.

"Of course he'll forget by tomorrow," I insisted, but Colette knew he wouldn't.

"Has he ever let us down?" she said.

Not then, not ever.

The next morning, very early, she came padding into my room in her terry-cloth bathrobe.

"Do you think he'll remember?" I asked, turning on the light. It was a test; I wanted to find out if the light dissolved the dream.

"Sure," Colette said confidently. "I can't imagine him lying to us."

She perched on the edge of my bed, and we waited for the rest of the house to rise. Robins chirped outside my window, as they'd been doing for years. I moved skittishly under the sheets. Every time I thought of him a little jolt went up my back, ending in a shiver. Colette hugged me saying, "It's the best thing that could ever happen, and we're in it together."

At last the doorbell rang, and we knew it was Yoshi. It was the first time he had ever called on us.

Sam answered, clutching her crimson housecoat at the neck, and ushered him into the living-room.

"Won't you sit down, Mr. Takahashi?"

We could tell by her quick movements she was excited to have him there.

"No time," he said, smiling and giving a short bow. Then he explained his plan for us.

Sam listened, stunned.

We could attend the orchestra rehearsals and the reception. "I rent them suite in Hotel Champlain," he said, not blinking an eye. "I pay for everything—no problem." He spread out his hands.

Sam nodded. "It sounds wonderful. I know the girls are thrilled."

We blushed.

"I'll just consult with my husband."

When she left the room I eyed Yoshi to see if there was a sign, even a wink, to indicate he remembered the nearness of our bodies. He made a remark about the weather. From the other room came sounds of whispering. It never occurred to me the answer might be no.

Sam returned, beaming. "My husband says that it's fine, and, Mr. Takahashi, you're a generous, charming man and we'll miss having you in the neighbourhood."

"I miss it too," he said, and they shook hands.

It was settled. We watched Yoshi disappear in an airline limousine, then we stared at each other barely daring to breathe.

"*This is it*," Colette said tautly, clutching her elbows in a criss-cross.

Sam began to bustle around the house. "You girls will have to make a quick trip to Simpsons—neither of you has decent coats or shoes. Come on now. Snap to it!"

As she spread the plaid suitcase open on the bed I suddenly realized she'd give anything to be going herself.

As we waved farewell to Father he said, in a half-hearted

Japanese accent, "You girls have velly good time."

Sam drove us down to Union Station, made sure the tickets had been reserved, then said, "Enjoy yourselves, girls."

She kissed each of us on the forehead, twice. Something in that gesture made me think she'd guessed what was going on.

□

"D'you think it's all right to leave him alone?"

The sand, now hours without sun, is cool between Jean's toes.

They look back at him, flat out on the ground, his belly rising and falling like some volcanic disturbance.

"Sure, why not?"

They walk parallel to the shoreline, silently, content to listen to the waves lapping near their feet and occasional cars swinging along the beach road. Colette strides, her long legs marking out a stork's path.

We are physically so unalike, Jean marvels. Everyone says: "Of course Colette takes after her *father*." The rest of the equation is left dangling.

Sea-rusted air salts her lips and she licks them. She hops over a sand castle someone has built, its moat now overflowing and the water destroying the curtain wall. Are the king and queen holed up in the keep, desperate for their lives as they peep out at the darkening world? Do they stare back into the bare room with its one lean potato and half bucket of drinking water?

Through her thoughts rises a new sound, unnameable. Maybe just ringing in her ears; it's been a long day. Her attention jerks to Colette. Her sister's hands dig into the front pockets of her jeans, rigid as wings.

The sound is like sobbing. It draws Jean in like a natural force, and she drops an arm over Colette's broad shoulders.

110

"What's happening?"

Her own voice is hoarse.

The answer is forever in coming.

"Nothing . . . really."

As if realizing how silly this sounds, Colette laughs through her crying, a congested noise. "I'm sorry, I didn't mean to get all sappy."

"Don't apologize – please."

They walk on, matching pace.

"It's just – " A deep breath. "Nelson. I don't know what the hell's going on." Colette shakes the words out as if they have been bunching in her head all day.

"I know this sounds ridiculous, but whenever I'm away from him I start doubting. How do I know if he's the right guy? What if I've blown it?"

Jean is determined not to show surprise.

"What makes you doubt?" She is calm and attentive. The world has closed to this little dark room, and she is immensely proud.

"Everything!" Another dull laugh. "We're constantly having misunderstandings and can't talk about them because . . . because any explanation would be misunderstood. That doesn't make sense." Colette stops talking and pulls out a handkerchief to blow her nose. "You know, sometimes I think we should have married each other, Jean. Think how it would simplify life – we could just go on as we had."

"Yeah, sure," says Jean. Suddenly she feels jittery. "Walk off into the sunset. The Mackenzie sisters."

"That's very good!" Colette loops an arm around Jean's waist. "You'd have to return to the Great White North."

"Just like that."

"Just like that. I suppose I could divorce Nelson."

"I don't get it." Jean pulls away. She's shivering. "Why are you saying all this? What do you want me to do? Take you seriously?"

"Oh, I'm serious," replies Colette. "You better believe it."

They reach a point where the beach narrows as it rounds the cliff.

"Sit for a moment?" says Jean.

They find a log and straddle it.

"The first time I met Nelson I had an infected pimple inside my nose," says Colette. "I was sure I looked like the Creature from the Lost Lagoon. The only reason I risked discovery was for a John Cage concert."

"I saw him once," inserts Jean. "He gave a performance at the Kitchen, on Broome Street. There were all these video screens and . . . "

"What was Nelson doing at a John Cage concert?" Colette puzzles aloud. She bends over and rests her elbows on her knees. "That's right: he just came along for the reception at the Schwitzers. He has sharp antennae for free booze. I almost didn't go, I felt so lousy about my nose."

"Was it that bad?"

"In my mind it was. In reality?" Colette lifts her palm. "Some redness, a little swelling. After the concert I hitched a ride with some other students to the renovated house in Cabbagetown: Professor Schwitzer's husband was a big-shot neurologist. Don't you always feel safe around doctors? I walked into the crowded room, and I tell you, Jean, the energy was like opening night on Broadway – not that I've ever been," she adds hastily. "I even met Cage for an instant, and he clasped my hand in that energetic American way looking me straight in the eye."

"And what did you say?"

"I babbled something then backed off quick as I could."

"That was dumb. Why didn't you start up a conversation?" Not that *she* had that evening at the Kitchen. Almost did, but at the last moment chickened out, having rehearsed her opening line so often it sounded like gibberish.

Colette shakes her head vigorously. "No way. A man I didn't know was propped up in the corner by the wine and cheese. When I found myself alone and trying to look like I'd planned it that way, I received a signal — a big wink followed by a smile that sent me wandering over to the table in search of a drink. You know Nelson's smile?" She looks anxiously at her sister.

"A fabulous smile," agrees Jean. She squints and peers down the beach at the black mass that must be Cody. So alone and still that a gull might mistake him for a log.

"I've probably told you this already, how we met," Colette continues eagerly. "He held out a hand saying, 'Hello, I'm Nelson Church. So you've met the great man, and what on earth have you done to your nose?' "

"He said that? How horrid."

Actually Jean has heard other versions of this story, but each time it's a little different, depending on Colette's mood. Sometimes she has herself speaking the opening line.

"No, it was a relief. Being found out is always a relief. I started discussing the concert, and it took five or ten minutes before I realized he hadn't been there. 'Why didn't you tell me?' I said, feeling dumb. He said, 'I like it better this way.' " Colette imitates the exact tones of the exchange.

It's strong for her, thinks Jean. Big as anything, big as the moon, big as the sky. Big as Yoshi. Big as me.

"Later that night," Colette continues dreamily, "it was dark, of course, and he walked me home across town. I remember when we stopped, somehow agreeing on it, and his hand touched my face. He pressed me against a cement wall far from the streetlight."

Her voice is lower and more intense. "I was where? Didn't know, never been there before. This wasn't Yoshi, or anything to do with him. And you weren't in the picture anywhere, Jean. The wool of his sweater scratched my skin." Colette laughs abruptly, then points in the air. "See, his face was only *his* face, his body only *his* body. So, he stayed. Moved into my apartment, spread his stuff around, and finally I'd found someone big enough. I knew I had to keep him."

"What more do you want?"

Colette sighs. "Reassurance? He hates it, clinginess. Drives him crazy. I have to be careful."

"Colette—What's that?" Jean points down the beach. There, marching steadily toward the water, is the shape of a giant teardrop.

"My God, it's Cody. He's heading for the sea!"

It's difficult to run in sand; like crossing the street in a dream. As they approach, Cody is wading naked into the chilly water, each step setting him off balance. His arms windmill the air.

Colette starts giggling. "If he falls he'll sober up fast."

"Or have a heart attack and drown; it's damn cold."

"Co-dy!" calls Colette.

The shape stops for a moment, and he puts his hands on his hips.

The sisters reach the shoreline a few feet away.

"What on earth are you doing?" exclaims Jean. "Do you want to get hypothermia?" She dips her toe into the water and shivers.

They hear something that sounds like moaning then turns into a song.

Cody, round and naked, stands knee-high in the Pacific Ocean singing:

"Life is like
A mountain railway
With an engineer so brave . . . "

"Cody, please. Come and put your clothes on." Colette sounds like an impatient mother.

His cock, perhaps because of the chill, is half-aroused. Jean stares. It seems so close, so easy and unmysterious, like a finger.

At last he totters in, bending and swinging to counter-balance the press of waves and undertow.

"From the cradle
To the grave . . ."

He sings exuberantly, like someone who has just discovered his voice after years of whispering in small apartments. He steps onto the sand and shakes, spraying them with water.

"That's bloody cold," he bellows. "I didn't see one god-damn fish. You'd think in an ocean this size there'd be fish, wouldn't you?"

Jean nods. They've been hours out there, and she's chilled to the bone.

Cody starts to look about, presumably for his clothes.

"Over there." Colette points to a heap by the rock.

"Where's my castle?" he says.

"Castle?"

"I built it earlier in the day: a lovely Rhine castle, an exact replica of one built by a Flemish nobleman. Seen it?" He steps backward then looks down at himself for the first time.

"I don't have any clothes on."

Jean picks up his things and tosses them over to him. "Get dressed, then we can look for your castle."

"Okay," he says agreeably.

They watch as he fumbles with the trousers, trying to separate front from back and inside from outside. He is laughing at his own confusion.

"Clothes? Yes ma'am, sure I can get dressed, learned to do it years ago. Tie laces, zip zippers, I can do it all." He plunges one foot into a leg and hops about. "Even tie flies! Come on, women. Help me, will ya?"

Jean lets him lean on her shoulder as Colette guides his foot into the leg. He has dispensed with underwear, or maybe never had any. His skin is cold and bumpy.

They all hop about now, like some five-legged race.

"Free me, free me!" he cries, parodying himself. "I'm overtaken with lust!"

He breaks away and leaps onto a rock and wails, "I NEED A WOMAN!"

Colette, doubled up with laughter, wraps an arm around Jean's waist.

"He thinks he's in *Amarcord*," she whispers, then cries out, "Here we are!"

Jean stiffens. She feels the hand dig into her hip, pressing her forward. "What are you doing?" she says in a low voice.

"Oh, loosen up, Jean."

She breaks away.

"I WANT A WOMAN!"

"It's not funny any more; can't you see he's just drunk?"

"So am I."

"Well, I'm not," says Jean. "He better watch it or he'll catch pneumonia."

Ignoring this, Colette moves toward Cody.

"Wait!" Jean follows.

He has slid off his perch and now sits, head drooping toward his knees, sighing deeply.

Jean forces a cheery tone. "I hope you aren't going to be sick."

I sound like a nurse, she thinks. She hates the little tremolo in her voice.

Colette kneels beside Cody and rests her temple against his shoulder. Water drips over her eyes.

"Co-dy," she croons. "Wa-ake up."

His hand drops sluglike over her shoulders. "I can't."

"Yes, you can," continues Colette in a teasing voice. She tickles him under the rib cage until he starts to giggle, a rattling sound like a motor that won't catch.

Jean feels a stab of something—envy? Envy of what? She stands before them bouncing up and down on her toes.

His trousers are half fastened and slide over his hips. He doesn't notice or care. His belly hangs over the waistband, a ridge of hair crowning it like a Mohican.

"I feel lousy," he moans, and sags even further.

"We'll have to help him up," Colette says. "Look, he's shivering like crazy. Dumb goof."

"I'm beat," he admits. "Can't make those stairs."

"We'll give you a hand," says Jean. She begins to plot the course of action. Colette will lead, and she will bring up the rear.

She rolls up her sleeves, not noticing the cold any more.

□

We were in the back seat of a Montreal cab late at night. Yoshi sat in the middle, and we huddled on either side in our stiff new clothes.

The concert was over. The reception was over.

"Where can I buy liquor?" Yoshi asked the cabbie.

I was shocked. "It's past two A.M., Yoshi, nothing's open."

"No wine anywhere?" he said in amazement.

But the driver said, "I think I can help you," and made a U-turn on the dark street.

I was nervous; something illegal was going to happen.

We steered down a back alley where garbage cans lay upended among the trash, and I'm sure I spotted a rat darting into a sewer grate.

The car stopped.

"This is it," the cabbie said, pointing to the rear of a tenement. Metal grates were slid across all the windows. "Want to come with me?"

"I come," said Yoshi, and squeezed out past us.

I wanted to say, "No, don't go," but the two men disappeared down some concrete steps into a basement.

"Listen—" Colette jostled me. "A secret knock." She sounded thrilled.

She was right. The cabbie rapped a distinctive signal, and we heard the clinking of metal and a door opening. Muffled male voices.

"Oh, God," I moaned. "What if they don't come back?" I imagined us abandoned in this bleak alley to rival gangs and armies of giant rats.

"A bootlegger," Colette whistled. "A bootlegger!" She had to say it again.

"I don't know about this," I said. "What if they get caught? We could all go to jail."

"Don't be such a stiff!" She gave me a playful push into the upholstery.

She didn't understand the possible danger, the grave consequences.

It seemed they were in there forever.

I kept peering up and down the alley for what I was sure would come—a car with a blinking red cherry, men with flashlights and a bullhorn.

There was a sound—the metal grate again—followed by footsteps. Yoshi hailed us, a wide grin on his face and a paper bag under his arm.

When he slipped back into his seat he gave my knee a squeeze.

"Jean looks so *worried*," he said.

The car spun off into the early morning blackness, back to the hotel suite and our suitcase full of brand-new clothes. Back to anything.

118

Chapter Nine

"I phoned Nelson." Colette places the rented fork on the rented tablecloth.

They are inside a giant tent, which was pitched that morning as they slept. The canvas billows royal blue, softened inside by a string of low-watt lightbulbs.

"Little fork, big fork," recites Jean, following Sam's instructions. "Knife, and spoon like so . . . " She looks critically at the scheme. She pushes the outer fork aside a centimetre, then pauses and looks at the larger arrangement. "So you phoned Nelson. What's he up to this Sunday?"

"He'd just been to the Dairy restaurant on Spadina for breakfast. He says he misses me."

"That's nice."

"Yeah." Colette slides onto a chair and places the box of cutlery on her lap. "When I hear his voice I realize I've had a boxing mitt over my body these past few days. They're doing a special issue on censorship for Freedom to Read week. He's really excited; actually, it's all he wanted to talk about." She yawns noisily. "We couldn't have got more than five hours' sleep, Jean. Think we'll make it?"

"We have to."

They are interrupted by a loud salute.

"Hello, girls!"

"Uh-oh," murmurs Colette. "Uncle Charlie and Aunt Ruth."

A tanned middle-aged couple approaches. The portly Uncle Charlie smiles broadly and claps his hands.

"We've come to view the operations!"

"You've come to the right place!"

"How are you, my dears?" Aunt Ruth, plump and pant-suited, reaches to give each sister a peck on the cheek. "Aren't you looking grand. And isn't this lovely! What a magnificent tent. I hope you're taking note of this, Charlie. I want one on our anniversary."

He ignores this. "You still in the Big Apple, Jeannie?"

"Sure am."

"Ruth and I went there once, right after we were married. We'd come back from Europe on the *Queen Elizabeth* and docked in New York City. A long time ago."

"We stayed at the hotel near the park," pipes up Ruth.

"That's right—the Plaza. Ever been there?"

Jean smiles no.

"Your weak-kneed aunt wouldn't go up the Empire State Building, so I had to go on my own."

"Oh, Charlie!" his wife protests. "It wasn't like that at all." She turns to the sisters and explains. "He didn't even ask me. I was conked out in the hotel room after too many martinis, so off goes King Kong here without so much as a by your leave."

"What do you think of the new house?" interjects Colette.

"Oh, it's lovely!" exclaims Aunt Ruth. "Your mother just took us on the grand tour. Everything's built from local materials, she said—isn't that right, dear?" She turns to her husband for confirmation.

"That's what she said."

Aunt Ruth wrinkles her brow. "I don't know that I'd want to be so far away from things—just speaking personally. We like to be handy to restaurants and the shows."

"Which reminds me," says Uncle Charlie. "You girls must visit us in Calgary. There's plenty of room in the house, and we'll show you all the hot spots. That is, if I can tear your aunt away from the basement still."

"Charlie!" Ruth turns to the sisters. "I'm making wine from a kit, and he's always making out that I'm some kind of hillbilly."

"Have you been to the beach yet?" asks Jean.

"No time. We just got here. Where is it?"

"Down those steps. You can hear the waves."

"My shoes!" exclaims Aunt Ruth.

They all look at her feet.

"Didn't you bring anything without heels, Ruth?"

"I'm afraid not. But you go, Charlie. I'll stay here and help the girls."

Charlie wraps an arm around his wife's waist and whispers into her ear.

"We're taking a stroll," he announces. "May as well appreciate all this fancy landscaping. Don't you girls work too hard. *Hasta luego*, as they say in Me-hico."

"See you later." Everyone waves.

When they have gone, Jean says, "Sam will have a fit; did you notice Charlie's wearing white loafers?"

"I noticed. She won't let him; he'll have to borrow something."

"Otherwise they're looking great, exactly as I remember them."

"They're always the same—thank God." Colette plays a balancing game with the box of cutlery. It teeters on her knee, threatening to slide off any minute.

Jean watches and sighs. "Such nice people."

"Yeah," says Colette. "Nice."

"No, I mean it; they're nice."

"I agree, Jean. Nice."

They convulse into laughter, dropping the stainless steel in a clatter on the ground.

◻

Long Lance, Blackfoot Indian, soon to become Brave, slashed the skin of his chest in two places so it made a flap. The chief threaded a rope under the flap and knotted it to the top of a pole about fifteen feet away. The Sun Dance began. As the drums beat and the elders began their chant, Long Lance danced, wrenching for hours under blazing sun at the rope attached to his chest. When it finally pulled free dragging a chunk of flesh with it, the young man was exhausted and near dead. He was now a Brave of the Blackfoot tribe.

"Read it again, Colette!"

"I don't know if I can."

The book had a worn red cover, and no one else ever signed it out of the school library. We were obsessed with it. We felt a kinship with Long Lance, a boy not much older than ourselves.

"Could you do it if you had to?"

The question ached at us. We half wished for a comparable challenge. One afternoon we decided to invent one: we would pierce our ears.

After locking ourselves in the upstairs bathroom we sterilized a darning needle.

"You have to do it to yourself; that's the way," I said.

Colette held the weapon in the flame until she burned her fingers, while I prepared the surface of her ear lobe with rubbing alcohol. Her heartbeat sent the vein on her temple into a little jag.

"What about you, Jean?" she asked anxiously.

"I'll do it after. Hurry up."

We could hear father's quartet practising in the studio below, like a giant bellows wheezing in and out.

I could tell she wouldn't do it if I indicated nervousness.

"Hold your ear and set the needle against it."

Grim faced, she obeyed.

"Now."

Her first jab was tentative. None the less she gave a squeal of pain.

"Come on, that couldn't have hurt."

She gazed at me defensively. "How do you know? I don't see you trying it."

"You're first, we already decided that."

"I hate pain."

But she gave it another go, this time pricking the skin and drawing blood. I felt my knees go jittery.

"Has it gone through?" she whispered.

"Nowhere near, but–" I hastily revised the plan. "Maybe it's enough. You've proven your bravery. See–there's blood."

"Blood?" She dabbed at it with her finger. "You're right; it's good enough."

Cheerily she stood up and made room for me on the toilet seat.

"Wipe off the needle and run it through the candle."

She obeyed, and though I was stalling for time she appeared not to notice.

With the needle pressed against the stinging surface of my ear lobe I felt like someone shooting up for the first time. Self-inflicted pain was the beginning of the swift descent into hell. But what about Long Lance? Pain brought enlightenment, too. Colette looked on impatiently. Somewhere far off the quartet took a turn and stampeded down the alley—a quick-footed, scherzo accompaniment to my sudden movement.

"There!"

"Jean! You've pushed it through your ear!" A hand shot to Colette's mouth. "I think I'm going to be sick."

So was I. But Long Lance rallied to the instant, casually sliding the needle through the lobe and out the other side, like a porcupine quill. Colette was looking at me with awe.

"I don't believe you did that. Doesn't it hurt?"

"No," I intoned in my young brave's voice.

Nothing hurt; I didn't feel a thing. Even the music had become a faint buzz. I was ready to hunt the great buffalo.

◻

"I'll be in my studio," Martin announces.

"As usual," mutters Jean. She's waiting for a bathroom to be free. The house is filled with out-of-town guests milling about, vibrating the house with their high heels and noisy greetings. Every faucet is turned full blast, each outlet plugged with a hair dryer, electric shaver, or curling iron. In the kitchen a plump woman sits on a stool and gulps instant coffee.

Above it all, like a siren, Lotte Lenya sings an explosive "Mack the Knife", jittering the rows of glass and crystal on the sideboard.

"If you're feeling rattled," suggests Martin, "join me."

Jean pulls the dressing-gown around her middle. It's been years since she's worn terry cloth—so nubbly and snug, with the vague aroma of Christmas mornings.

"Maybe I will."

She follows him down two carpeted steps. As the door shuts behind them the room fills with silence.

124

"That sounds great," she says.

Martin nods, but doesn't sit. Instead he links hands behind his back and strolls over to the window.

"Weather's holding up," he notes.

"Uh-huh. So far."

"Certainly are a lot of people about."

"Feels like a hundred!"

"I wish . . . " he begins. "I wish they'd all go home."

"Dad!"

"No, really." He pivots and boosts himself onto the window ledge. "I wanted this to be a family affair, but your mother . . . " He trails off.

"I know."

He smiles. "She says it snowballed, got beyond her control, but I doubt that. The only thing that keeps me sane is knowing she's in perfect control."

Jean squirms uncomfortably. For a moment she envisions a horrifying confidence: "Your mother and I have not been happy together . . . did you know we've taken to sleeping in separate beds . . . our sexual life isn't all . . . "

Instead Martin rubs his hands together.

"Want to play a duet?"

Jean jerks to attention.

"Calm our nerves," adds Martin. "I still have your old student cello in the closet. It gets used every so often, so I guarantee the strings aren't rotten."

This last bit is spoken from inside the wall closet. He emerges, grinning, carrying her old cello by the scruff of the neck. Its varnish looks cheap and is chipping at the edges.

"Don't scowl; I've seen worse. Surely you feel a trace of sentiment for your first instrument?"

"Not really." Jean automatically holds out her hand for it and pulls up a stool. She wrinkles her nose. "Phew, mothballs!"

"Your mother keeps blankets in there. Is it too bad?"

He watches her anxiously. "You can use mine if you like."

"Oh no, this is fine."

Maybe I can get through this without him noticing, she hopes. Just play what the notes say and think about something else.

Martin pushes a stand toward her and starts going through a pile of scores, licking his thumb and darting through book after book.

"Aha!" Triumphant, he lifts out a single folded sheet. "You'll like this – very modern!"

When he hands it to her she reads the cover: "Brandão: 'Two Close Fits'. What's this?"

Martin's eyes shine. "Just you wait; this guy's terrific. It's exactly what the title says; we're always on top of each other, poking in and out of each other's part. A close fit. Come on, Jeannie." He raps his bow on the stand. "Let's get started. Shoot me an 'A'."

The notes bounce all over the page like a shower of cigarette burns. Even when she squints, the staff lines all run into each other.

She runs the bow over the top string. Down a full tone and a half. The tone raw as a freshly skinned knee.

As she reaches to twist the peg it begins: the nausea. Regular as morning sickness. Even the smell of the varnish makes her gag.

"I can't do it," she says.

"What do you mean?" He doesn't understand yet. He is still poised eagerly on the edge of his chair, bow hovering over the strings.

She flops back on the stool.

"I – I'm not playing much these days."

"Oh?" His eyes narrow into dime slots.

"Don't look so disapproving. I just don't see the point of it any more."

"Point of what?" His smile is forced now.

126

Her voice trembles. "I don't know how *you* can keep doing it year after year. How long's it been, forty-five years? *God.*"

She gives a snort of disgust. "I mean, you make the same bloody racket, maybe play one section a little better one day, dig hidden nuances out of a phrase that probably doesn't deserve it—"

"Whoa!" He flattens a hand in the air. "You're dead serious, chum. But don't get angry at me."

"Why not? That's exactly what you're like—isn't it?" She lays the cello on the floor, clumsily, so it makes a loud "bonk" of wood against wood. Martin winces. Other sounds have begun to seep into the room: laughter, the shutting of doors, the drone of Kurt Weill.

She goes back to sink into the soft couch and closes her eyes. She can hear him moving about: replacing the instrument in the case with a soft almost transparent thud.

A hand touches her shoulder.

"Jean," he says. "I think I know what's going on, believe it or not. You're not the first to have a crisis of faith."

"What do you mean?"

He drops beside her on the couch.

"That's the life's work," he says, with a little nervous laugh. "I don't know how else to explain it."

"There's nothing *to* explain." She hears her voice, a hollow, melodramatic "clink".

He pauses a moment. "See, musicians have to answer that question every day, each time we put music in the air. Or, at least, the smart ones pose the question. It makes us try harder, keeps us from relaxing or getting complacent. Believe me, Jean, it's a life's work."

Slowly she turns to face him.

"Are you trying to tell me that it's a life's work trying to stretch music into a life's work?"

"Sort of."

"That's nuts!" She tries to read his face, but he's staring blandly at the ceiling. "You can't say that!"

"It's a shock to find the emperor has no clothes," he admits. His voice gathers momentum. "Then it's a relief – even exciting. You'll see. It's your job, our job, to invent new clothes daily – "

"What do you mean, 'clothes'? I'm not a dress designer!"

He eyes her curiously. "Something's happened to yank the fantasy out from under you. I don't know what" – he shakes his head – "and I don't care. It makes me sad. I guess I thought maybe you could keep going with it, like some forest creature, like Pan – "

Jean scowls.

Ignoring this, he continues. "The important thing is that you keep at it, even after you discover no one much cares."

"That's just it!" cries Jean. "I feel like one hand clapping!"

"Better one than none. After all" – his hand whirls in the air – "it's only a cello. A curvy box with strings stretched over it. It's not a witch's broomstick, Jean, or a magic carpet. It's not going to make you other than you are."

Jean stares at him. "You've figured all this out before."

"Of course. As you pointed out, I've been at this nearly forty-five years."

"I'm not sure I want to understand what you're saying."

"Good, good," he urges. "Never get over it and you might be a smart musician."

"I don't know, it sounds crazy."

"Of course!" He nods passionately. "There's really nothing there. Music, sound; it disappears so fast that you're bound to spend your life chasing it."

Suddenly Jean feels deeply uneasy. It's like when she first realized that Sam was as terrified of thunderstorms as she was; that when, as little girls, she and Colette sneaked under the covers of their parents' bed they were lending as much comfort as they were receiving.

"It sounds like you *enjoy* it," says Jean slowly. She feels a soft spray of excitement.

"But I do!" He is gleeful now, tugging her shoulder in close to him.

His laughter begins as a gentle trickle, then gradually swells into a tumbling cataract. Soon Jean joins in; she can't help it. Before long everything's laughing: her toes, knees, fingers, kidneys, all giggling together like a girls' pajama party.

Guests start to swarm. On the hall table a stack of telegrams grows. Flowers from absent guests arrive.

"Maybe we can use these for the tables," suggests Colette, sniffing an ample bouquet of tiger lilies.

People seem to know what to do. Bars have been set up around the rim of the tent, and roving waitresses carry trays of canapés. Guests prowl with glasses full of wine or Perrier water. They deposit themselves in odd spots – a rock on the edge of the garden stream, the crook of a branch, a car bumper.

Cars jam the driveway and form a line down the road as far as the eye can see. In front is a beat-up white convertible with New York license plates: Cody's.

New arrivals carry brightly wrapped boxes into the house. These are deposited in a neat pile on the fireplace by a student who has been hired to direct traffic and discreetly check names off a list. Jean and Colette circulate, prompting remarks like: "Isn't that the girl I used to see playing scrub baseball in the park?"

Jean feels her freshly washed hair shimmer under the sun's glow.

Colette is wearing fuchsia silk pants with a turquoise shell. As the breeze catches the material it flutters lazily, pressing over hips and collarbone. It's the first time since arrival she's been out of survival gear.

Jean has squeezed into a near miniskirt, burgundy. In New York all the downtown women wear them. But here...?

Staring at herself in the full-length mirror an hour ago, she was appalled. She pressed her nose to the glass and examined the tributaries that trailed off from her eyes. It could just be the light. She smiled and the lines deepened. As an infant she used to squeeze up her face and scream for hours, for no apparent reason.

She wished there was time for a long, relaxing bath. All afternoon there was a race for the showers and the limited hot-water supply. The overnight guests milled about in various stages of undress. It was like being backstage at an amateur operatic production. People helped each other with zippers and hair.

Colette said, staring into the mirror, "Can I get away with this belt?"

"Too heavy, it drags down the material."

Jean began to apply lipstick and eyeshadow while her sister watched, amused.

She passed on the lipstick, Clinique's Rosy Plum, and Colette stroked it on with ease. The colour suited her better. Then she said, "You know, Jean, I always feel like a female impersonator when I do this."

Jean understood right away. Whenever she's in a public washroom and emerges from the cubicle to see women standing before the mirror with open compacts, little brushes and pencils, saucers of paint, she flashes one look at the mirror and gets the hell out. She doesn't belong, not with those women so comfortable with the articles of femaleness.

Some guests look familiar. Jean acknowledges tentative smiles.

"Are you Martin and Samantha's daughter?"

"Which one might you be, the one in Toronto or New York?"

"I love your miniskirt, dear. I only wish I were young and thin enough." (This said by a woman not three years older and certainly five pounds lighter than Jean.)

"Isn't this house delightful? You must be very proud."

Jean smiles and continues to stroll over the grass. She sets herself goals: over to that red Toyota, turn, walk casually to the Johnny-on-the-Spot, circle it, stare distractedly at the sky, continue back to the tent entrance.

How's Colette doing? she wonders. She'd run off saying, "We mustn't stick together." There she is cradling an empty glass, moving her face in eager chatter as she touches the arm of a man in an olive suit. Her new friend suggests something, then takes the empty glass. With the other hand he brushes Colette's elbow, and they saunter off together toward the bar.

There's not a woman in sight with a skirt above the knee. God, what a mistake. Wasn't it Margaret Trudeau who scandalized the continent by wearing a short dress to a White House function?

Where's Cody? He's been lying low all day, no doubt nursing a fierce hangover. Not a sign of his rotund form. No bearded men here–unless you count the professorial chap with the neat goatee.

Jean likes to think of herself as socially "ept". In New York she often breaks the ice with a warm or witty remark. People say she's a natural.

Despite prickles of sweat under her arms she feels neither warm nor witty nor natural, and her drink has just run out. This provides an excellent opportunity for purposeful action. She strides across the neat crewcut of grass, over a gently rolling hill to one of the bars.

"That hill," noted her father earlier, "is man-made."

The bar is tended by two young men in crisp white shirts

and black chinos. A row of blenders roars on the counter top, producing a supply of the cocktail for the occasion: the Hopper. Jean orders one, and watches the green froth spill into a tall, frosted glass.

"Know what that stuff looks like to me?" winks the bartender. He's one of Martin's students.

"I don't want to hear." She leans against the counter and faces out. Where's Colette gone with the young man?

Over there, backed against the canvas tent. He's so square, thinks Jean. Not Colette's type at all. He even has a nervous tic: every minute or so he adjusts the handkerchief in his vest pocket with a quick pat. He probably has one of those beepers hitched to his belt.

Jean almost strolls across to join them, but something holds her back. Perhaps it's pleasant enough where she is, on a ridge where she has a clear view of everything.

◻

When the Davises moved next door to Number 201, the little brick cottage, I took over a tinfoil container of my famous walnut squares. I wanted to meet the new people before anyone else. Maybe I should have consulted Colette and we could have done it together, the baking, the presentation, just like old times.

Diane and Randy had style. They were thirtyish. He wore narrow-cut leather jeans from England, and she refused to wear skirts. Best of all they seemed to find me interesting. We sat around for hours gabbing, and they asked all about my life – thus far. I was so flattered that my lips became rubbery, flexible, and I told all. Even about Colette and me and Yoshi and, if this constituted a betrayal, they were charmed by the tale and let themselves be sworn to secrecy. I told them about Montreal, about how the bellboy came in that morning with a message and saw the three of us lying on the mattresses on the floor, the sheets skewed.

And how Yoshi reached up and took the message with just a towel wrapped around his waist.

Randy kept saying, "What did you do with him, Jean?" so I had to tell. They were so interested. I sat around their funky living-room (Afghani tapestries, pigskin chairs from Mexico, luxurious sheepskin rugs from Greece) sipping cool white wine from an immense beaker. Sometimes I took my cello over and played. They listened closely and afterwards exclaimed that I was destined for "great things".

One afternoon, Diane, a shapely nine-months pregnant, planned my future role as baby sitter.

"You'll get a dollar-fifty an hour," she said, and I grinned because that was double my usual rate.

"And when we go up to the lake you'll have to come and swim and drink gin-and-tonics and meet the cute counsellors from the tennis camp."

"Sure," I nodded. "I'll do that."

"All our friends have cottages around the lake. It's a chaotic social scene: Peyton Place North."

Ahh, I breathed. It grew more interesting by the moment. But it was the Men, the thirty-year-old men, that attracted me far more than boy camp counsellors. Giggling, I dared tell them so.

"Jean!"

"Don't you like boys your own age?" prodded Randy, pouring me another drink.

"They're all right," I yawned, watching him fill the glass. He hadn't shaved for two days and the stubble made him look European.

The perfect baby was finally born, and everything came to pass as planned. Now and then Colette realized I was up to something, when I disappeared for long weekends or came home with liquor breath, but we didn't discuss it, except in passing.

"Randy thinks I should try out for the youth orchestra," I said one day. "He thinks I'm good enough."

"Oh yeah?" Colette didn't take her head out of the book.

I couldn't get her interested in them. When she referred to my friends at all she said, "Those people opposite Yoshi's house."

Yoshi had been in New York for months already.

Eventually the time came when Colette was to meet the Davises. It was Diane's idea; she wanted to meet my sister after all the stories they'd heard.

"I'll go if you want," Colette said.

She slipped into a pair of commando boots and tucked her jeans into the tops. She followed me next door without a word.

"I'm sure you'll like them," I chattered, but I smelt danger. We were barely through the introductions when Colette eyed the living-room and remarked, "Looks like just about every country is represented here." She picked up a clay dish from Bali. "Is this real?"

My breath stopped.

Diane and Randy exchanged glances, then brought out the fabled wine and the Perfect Child. The wine was poured into oversized glasses while baby Teresa rolled and gurgled on the sheepskin rug.

"She's quite a tubby little thing," Colette said after a few sips of Blue Nun had wet her tongue. "Her face looks a little mashed in — is that from the forceps?"

The room froze. Blushing, I stared at the floor and prayed for a natural catastrophe. Instead, Colette slipped out of her boot and extended her toes, nudging Baby Teresa.

"Gitchy-goo," she said in a flat voice. Then, "What on earth do you *do* with babies? They're hardly members of the human race."

There was a loud crack. Diane had slammed her goblet down on the glass table. She twirled the Greek bracelets around her wrist so fast they sang. Then she spoke in a low, contained voice I had never heard.

"Perhaps, Miss Hopper, we'd better have our little gathering some other time."

She stood up, and I followed suit, spilling wine on my Indian shirt. I was ready to carry Colette out, by the hair if necessary. The three of us closed around like secret-service men, ushering her to the door before more harm could be done. Randy turned to me pointedly and said, "We'll see you Friday night. Sixish?" and touched me lightly on the cheek with his hand.

"Sure," I mumbled, amazed he was still speaking to me.

At last the grey door closed behind us and did I hear a bolt slide across? Too tight-lipped to say a word I scampered down the limestone steps, leaving Colette as far behind as possible.

Later I watched her yank off the boots and line them up on the mat. She acted as if nothing had happened.

For some reason I began seeing less of Randy and Diane. Not that they were angry with me – but I seemed to lose interest in their baby and their furniture and even the wine.

"What happened to those people with the baby?" Colette asked later that summer as we hugged the red canoe in close to the shore. It was a long weekend at the Bay and the sky was ominous with clouds and dark growlings.

"Ah, yes." I affected a surprised laugh. "I'd totally forgotten about them."

Colette nodded, and her paddle continued its creaseless glide through water.

◻

"How are you making out?"

It's Cody, draining a beer. He must have raided the inside fridge.

Jean, grateful to see him, admits, "I don't know yet. How about you?"

He shrugs and smiles weakly. His loose-fitting safari jacket flops over a white shirt that is a size too small. People are watching him. With his shaved head and full beard he cuts an imposing figure.

"Just got up, to tell the truth." He stretches his arms and yawns, making no effort to cover his gaping mouth.

" 'Scuse me," he mutters. "Where's the food? I haven't had breakfast."

"It's not time yet."

"And Colette?"

Jean shoots a glance, and his gaze follows hers.

"She's found someone." He pats an inside pocket. "Care to smoke a joint?"

"Maybe later. I don't want to smell of it."

"There's your daddy, man of the hour."

They watch Martin cross the lawn. He is wearing a tan suit imported from a small house in Milan. Within seconds he is intercepted by two attractive women who swoop in, each clasping a tan elbow. There is the tinkle of feminine laughter.

"My father's good-looking," observes Jean.

Cody laughs shortly. "You bet."

"Do you think he has affairs?" She says it half jokingly.

"Want me to tell tales?"

"Of course!"

Cody clears his throat. "I doubt that he does anything more than that." He points with his eyes.

Martin is lifting two boiled prawns from a passing tray. He drops them, one by one, into the mouths of his consorts.

"Corny," says Jean.

"What did you expect?" Cody looks at her. "Do you think you're more inventive?"

"Probably not." She laughs confidently, knowing she is, just a little.

They move to a knob of hill near a drainage hole and

sit on the grass. Cody grunts as he lowers himself. Jean worries a moment about her skirt.

There are some wonderful smells coming from the cooking tent. Uniformed men dart in and out, carrying things. The party looks like it's working. No one is standing around alone, except to admire some feature of the landscaping. Sam is bustling about, lit up like a firefly. She is wearing a luminous dress, four layers of contrasting silks that cascade as she moves. When she descends upon a group she is greeted with affectionate kisses and exclamations of approval.

"Wonderful party, Samantha!"

"I'm so glad we could come."

"New York, eh?"

Jean jerks to attention. Cody is watching her.

"Yes. Four years now."

"What part?"

She tells him about her loft on the Bowery above the lighting store. How it's so loud at night she bought a "white noise" machine that imitates sounds of surf crashing in on shore.

He laughs. "You must feel right at home here, with real ocean."

They lie back, elbows on the grass. Jean peers down at her stockinged legs. They look good. They should: she shaved them this morning. Her skirt rides high, and this causes a moment of self-consciousness. She tugs at the hem while Cody grins, nodding his head.

"Nice legs."

"Yeah, thanks."

Martin waves from afar, cheerily lifting his glass. Cody doesn't notice him, but Jean waves back.

"Feel all right today? How's your head?"

"My head's okay," she says. "I wasn't that drunk."

137

"No? Wish I could say the same." He coughs unnecessarily. Jean realizes he's ill at ease. Perhaps he feels nervous now that they're alone.

He wets his lips, then wipes them with the back of his hand.

In that one gesture she sees it, the power she might wield. How could she have forgotten? The giant boxing mitt Colette spoke of. It peels off, and the new feeling hits her bloodstream fast.

"Let's arrange to meet in New York," he suggests. "Next Sunday for lunch. You choose a place."

"Okay." She thinks a moment—it all seems so far away. "How about Danielle's on Spring Street. You paying?"

He makes a face. "Sure."

"Then it's a deal. One P.M. at the bistro."

Her body stirs gently on the grass, rolling with the slope. She feels relieved already.

A group of women walk by, carrying long-stemmed glasses full of white wine. Sam insisted on real glass—no plastic. Snatches of conversation float through the air: they are speaking of Wittgenstein.

"That's Emily Lemmerich: Professor Emeritus at U. Vic," whispers Cody. "Big shot in the philosophy of language. She's over seventy now."

"Why is she in Victoria?"

"Likes the climate. Cambridge was too cold and damp."

"How do you know all this?" Jean pivots so their torsos are facing.

"I just do."

Colette and her friend are being joined by the group of distinguished women.

"And here I am," thinks Jean, "sitting on the dirt with the guy I drank with last night."

Then that old song comes bouncing into her head, "Love the One You're With", and she nearly laughs aloud. She's used it dozens of times, possibly hundreds, over the years.

"Tell me about your life in New York, Cody. What bars do you go to? What's your job like?"

He eyes her suspiciously; then, flattered, begins to answer. Every minute or so he checks that she's still attentive.

"You interested in this?" he asks for the third time. He's telling her about the Puerto Rican social club he once crashed by mistake.

"Sure."

He carries on, but she's got him now, drawing him with sure strokes, like a housewife yanking in the laundry.

His eyes are warm and brown, and watering from the sun.

He finishes – with a question, she realizes. She blinks and asks him to repeat it.

"Weren't listening," he accuses.

Then he places a hand over hers, pressing it to her nylon thigh.

At that instant Martin heads toward them, and Jean manages to glide her hand out.

"Your mother needs you," Martin says, after a quick glance at the retreating hands.

A gong rings three times and Jean springs to her feet.

Chapter Ten

"Drink up, my dear."

Uncle Charlie splashes wine into Jean's glass. He thinks she's not having enough fun. Under the head table his shoes have scuff marks where she shaved them with her own.

He points to a pale slab of meat on her plate. "What's this?"

"*Vitello tonnato.*"

Jean pokes at it without enthusiasm. The business with the feet started as an accident — "Oops, got a smudge on your whites!" Until the third time, when she accidentally brushed his instep and he reached under the table and clasped her stockinged ankle for longer than the joke required.

"What's the deal with the rice?" Uncle Charlie prods his, sniffing. "Is it supposed to be cold? I don't want to get ptomaine." He lets his yellow cuff dance through the sauce.

"Of course. It's a summer dish."

In the far corner of the tent a piano quintet dutifully plays, inaudible against the cacophony of voices and cutlery. Each time they finish a piece and let their bows drop, Sam applauds enthusiastically.

Jean and Colette are going to see Yoshi tomorrow.

Colette claims she doesn't want to. She hopes to dissuade Jean so she can slip off on her own. Jean won't let her.

Martin sits to Jean's left, the fork rarely meeting his lips. He doesn't like eating where he can be watched; a meal is a private act, like going to the toilet. French cuffs, meticulously laundered and cuff-linked, bear not a sign of spatter.

"Congratulations, Martin."

A woman sheathed in a pink dress leans over the head table to kiss his cheek. As she bends, her cleavage is inches from his face. Jean looks down at her plate.

"Thank you." He rises slightly from his chair and bows.

Imagine this, Colette, imagine if I feel *nothing*, Jean thinks. Or say I come down with all the old symptoms, like a bout of malaria, cold sweat and yammering heart, while Colette saunters in loose as Perry Como, hugging him, one old pal to another, letting fly a few witty remarks as my mouth forms only vowels . . .

"Why don't you go on your own, Jean?" Colette dropped an ash into a tall vase.

"Don't be absurd! It doesn't mean anything without both of us." Jean searched Colette's face for agreement and found the fast snapshot of irritation.

Is that Cody?

He cruises into view bold as can be and sits at a nearby table. Jean returns his toast, echoing the daring swoop of his wineglass.

There is a commotion behind her back.

"What's *he* doing there?"

Sam is leaning behind Martin, her face knotted in anger.

"I don't know. Does it matter?"

"Damn right it does. I have no intention of staring into that mug for the rest of the evening."

Cody beams angelically.

Suddenly, Jean wants to know. "Why do you care so much? What is it about him?"

Sam clamps down her lip and holds a beat.

Martin, hearing the whispers, twists in his chair and says, "What are you women conspiring about?"

Sam's grimace floats into a smile. "Wouldn't you like to know!"

Why doesn't she like Cody? Of course, she's always been appalled by overweight people. "There's a sight," she'll wince, straightening her spine. "That's what can happen."

Jean gazes down the red-frocked table at Colette and they exchange winks. Colette's hair, dark and shining, bristles on her head like animal fur. Surprisingly, she looks at ease in her silk, as if she didn't live in guerilla dress, those drab fatigues that make you realize *she* looks good in them but no one else would.

She leans on an elbow and speaks to Aunt Ruth. Her sleeve slips up to reveal a slender freckled wrist, a hand clasping a knife. She is about to penetrate the salmon.

Look out for bones, Colette. That fragile wrist. The thin membranes of your throat.

Aunt Ruth is laughing merrily. Later she'll tell Charlie, "Colette has become such a delightful young lady—and *funny*. I can't tell you when I've laughed so hard."

What can she be saying? Jean can't guess any more. The man Colette was with earlier has disappeared into the crowd, his olive suit melting in with dozens, everything turning blue under the canvas as twilight begins.

"This fish looks good enough to eat!" declares Uncle Charlie. He slips an arm around Jean's waist, squeezing, and could it be an accident that his fingertips graze her left breast?

"Let's have a go!" She recklessly stabs at his portion and lifts a chunk into her mouth.

His cheek presses against Jean's, and he mimics her chewing so they're like pistons moving up and down. His cheek is smooth and smells of Yardley's. It's a bit much, and Jean pulls away.

"You're quite a gal," Uncle Charlie says.

Jean knows this score by heart.

A sound begins, gentle at first, then building with a steady crescendo: the clatter of a hundred spoons knocking glass.

"SPEECH! SPEECH!"

Charlie pours more wine into the glass and, like a fool, Jean is drinking, aware of a hundred pairs of clucking, predatory eyes. The sound vacuums in and out. Charlie is shuffling through an inner pocket for a piece of paper. He rocks to his feet and clamps one hand on the tabletop.

"Ladies and gentlemen – friends." He clears his throat. The spoons stop their racket.

"I am not an orator," announces Charlie. "Nor a philosopher. But I am a great appreciator of those people more gifted than me."

"I!" hisses Sam.

Jean tries to catch Colette's eyes, but Colette's got them trained toward the peak of the tent.

"We are here to celebrate the continuing happiness of my sister, Samantha, and her husband, Martin, who has deigned to join us officially in the colonies."

Titters of laughter; Martin gamely joins in.

Charlie, who, as his wife insists, "has a way with an

143

audience when he gets the chance," waits a long moment – until the last chuckle has died – before he resumes.

"We are here to turn the sod on this beautiful house . . ."

"Wrong expression," Martin mutters. "It's long turned."

Oblivious, Charlie beams at his sister and brother-in-law.

"I guess the reason you made such a big house was so all your relatives from colder climes can visit in the winter!"

Sam acknowledges this with a show of mock horror.

"Pretty soon you'll be gardening, playing shuffleboard and bingo, and going to bed at nine so you can get up with the rooster . . . "

This time Jean makes a face.

"We're all delighted that Martin finally has a regular job, with a pension" – Charlie pauses meaningfully – "so we don't have to support him in his declining years."

The laughter is forced at this point. Waiting until the last snicker freezes, Charlie clears his throat before continuing in a more serious tone.

"When I was home in Calgary, ruminating on what I would say on this occasion, it soon became clear I had in the house someone who could say it far better." Charlie gallantly stretches a hand out toward his wife. A delighted blush creeps up Ruth's neck.

"So I said to my wife, 'Why don't you compose a verse especially for the occasion and I'll read it. That way we both get our two cents in!' "

As Ruth beams, her husband slips his bifocals over his nose and smooths the piece of paper. Looking over his arm Jean can see that the poem has been written in Gothic script, with elegant flourishes on upper-case letters. His hand shakes, and he begins to recite haltingly, as if it were a foreign language:

"As the peasant dips his plow into the damp, dark earth
You have planted seed . . . "

The two of us stood in over-sized navy choir gowns in the alto section of the Jubilee Singers. The percussion section was under my right toe, and the blond man who managed cymbals and snare kept winking at us between cues. "What are you doing here?" I knew he was thinking.

This was the big time: on stage at Massey Hall with the symphony orchestra and guest soloists. The work was Beethoven's Choral Fantasia, a crowd pleaser, with, coincidentally, Yoshi Takahashi at the keyboard. The conductor was a famous red-faced Englishman whom Father had gone to school with at the Juilliard, eons ago. How we got into this event is a story itself, especially considering I'd never been able to lift a tune let alone carry one.

When Yoshi saw us at rehearsal, singing our hearts out from the fifth row, he hardly blinked. By then nothing we did fazed him. At one point he was a fraction late in his entry, and Sir Charles Tisdell threw his hands up in the air and cried, "You should know, Yoshi, you should know!"

Yoshi bowed his head.

We squirmed.

Later, over chicken soup at Murray's, he told us that Sir Charles was an old teacher of his.

"For five years he is professor of orchestration at Conservatory in Tokyo where I go. He is still scary guy to me!"

Yoshi grinned and tore off a section of bread.

We swelled up with delight to be part of this. Our names were on the back of the program in tiny print. They spelt Colette's wrong: "Colt Hopper."

"Kid Colt," I laughed.

"How could they!" she cried and crumpled the sheet into a ball. There were tears in her eyes, which surprised me. It didn't seem like such a big thing.

Half an hour before performance time we hung around backstage in our choir gowns, rushing to the bathroom every ten minutes. It was, we'd been told, a sell-out crowd. At one point a reporter was hovering around with a heavily laden photographer in tow, snatching quick interviews with the soloists. A famous contralto beckoned me over and asked me to zip up her dress, which was several sizes too small, and I wondered what would happen when that extraordinary chest filled with air.

Nerves – did I have nerves – while Colette leaned languidly against a dirty pillar and told me to calm down. I was only fooled for a minute: her face was pale and her lips white from constant gnawing.

Where was Yoshi?

We knew he liked to arrive at the last minute, and there he was, bent over in a rush to the changing room, score under arm. Outside Massey Hall his name was printed in yard-high letters.

"Mr. Takahashi!" It was the reporter stumbling forward. "A moment of your time!"

Yoshi's face flashed annoyance, but he stopped and waited as the photographer took a light reading.

"Mr. Takahashi," the reporter chattered. "Most performers are superstitious and have some ritual they enact before stepping into the arena. Is there anything particular you do, like Bernstein kissing Koussevitzky's cuff-links?"

Yoshi brushed a lock of black hair from his forehead and looked baffled. I could tell he was having difficulty translating the question. At last he said slowly, "I have ritual too; everyone does."

The interviewer nodded encouragement. I noticed other people were listening with expectant smiles.

"My shoes." He pointed at the carefully shined yet worn oxfords on his feet. "Once they belong to fine pianist. He gave them to me in emergency – same size feet, almost – he's not a very big guy, so that night I play very well and I am not nervous about anything. So now I wear them always for concert; it is luck for me."

146

The reporter scribbled on his note pad, and a flash bulb went off. *Toronto Star*. Tomorrow I'd check it out.

Then Yoshi saw us. His round face lit up, and he waved both arms, in slow motion.

Everyone who was watching turned to look at us. I managed to mouth, "Hello."

"I get ready now." He bowed, then disappeared into the little room.

Minutes later, staring into the lip of the audience that filled Massey Hall to the rafters, the absurdity of it all tilted in like a funhouse mirror. Thousands of faces zoomed in on mine: the Great Imposter. They knew I was just mouthing the words, not daring to sing in my tuneless croak. My knees unlocked, and I practically keeled over, saved only by my neighbour, a hearty contralto. I was shivering and sweating all at once. I knew that I'd pass out if I didn't leave the scene, pronto; so, while throats sucked in for the choral entrance—"*Schmeichelnd. Schmeichelnd.*"—I sneaked along the aisle and edged between curtains, praying that I'd make it. Finding myself in the dark corridor leading to the greenroom I knelt down and put my head between my legs. It was supposed to help. Then I started to sob while, inches away, my colleagues filled the hall with the most glorious music in the world. I could envisage, with each crisp chord, Yoshi's head bucking up and down, making an arc of blue-black hair.

And Colette was still out there, perhaps not even noticing my absence, singing our hearts out.

◘

"And that's all I have to say, except to propose a toast." Charlie lifts his glass.

"To Martin and Samantha!"

Gulp.

"And peace in the world!"

147

Jean drinks up, hearing murmurs of "Isn't that nice," and gives Charlie a chaste kiss on the cheek as he sits, because it was much better than it might have been.

Colette signals from her end, "Good going, Uncle Charlie and Aunt Ruth!"

He is so pleased, blushing and trying not to. He flutters a hand toward his wife, including her in the acclaim.

Then Sam stands up, clearing her throat and gathering her sleeves into little bracelet-rolls. At first they can barely hear her as she begins to speak in a hoarse whisper. Her eyes are shot with tears. The piece of paper with her prepared speech lies discarded on the table. As the room settles, she begins again: a woman's voice, pitched high as it strains to be heard. Jean can smell Sam's perfume, a garden called "Tea Rose". She doesn't dare look at her mother's face, being too familiar with its flutter of nervous tension. Instead she clutches her wet napkin, coiling it into a red snake.

"It's been too long since we've been together like this . . ."

"We've *never* been together!" calls a voice from the crowd.

Sam nods graciously. "And it will occur again. Only" – she smiles – "it's someone else's turn. Get married, have an anniversary, win the Nobel Prize – anything."

She is greeted with chuckles.

"But don't lose touch. Champagne" – she lifts her glass level with her nose and examines it – "may be thicker than water, but blood is thicker than both by far. And we are *joined*, make no mistake," she says firmly. "This, us" – she makes eye contact with the now hushed crowd – "is a dynasty, of family and friends, both equally vital to the whole. To us!" She tips her glass.

"To us!"

"Now," she continues. "We are here to celebrate a very important act: my husband's official adoption of this country. You are from all over the continent. You know" – her voice cracks just a little – "what it is to be a patriot. Martin, too, is a patriot. Only because he feels, deeply feels, the importance of nationality has it taken so long for this metamorphosis to occur. It is no light thing."

"Jeez," Jean mutters to Uncle Charlie. "Only thirty years. What's the hurry?"

"And since it is his day, I have asked him to break the special news – later."

"Ohhh." There are groans of disappointment.

Sam sits back down in her chair, breathing shallowly. Her face is drained of colour. Despite Jean's best intentions her skin is crawling with curiosity.

"And now," Aunt Ruth rises to make a prearranged announcement. "We shall temporarily adjourn to the sweets table!"

Amidst the jostling Jean catches a signal from Colette.

"Meet you by the Gateaux St. Honoré."

Two long tables form an "L" at the south end of the tent. Spread on the white cloth are big platters containing an array of soft ripe cheeses, pungently expanding beyond their rinds. Beside them are bunches of grapes and nuts, tiny tarts filled with kiwi fruit, blueberries, and lemon, and what could only be the Gateaux St. Honoré. It's a huge construction of caramel-coloured balls attached to a perilous wooden scaffolding.

Jean grabs a plate and loads up with something of everything. The drunkenness has passed, and she feels mainly lightheaded and a bit frantic.

As Colette sidles up, munching a handful of grapes and nuts, they are descended upon by a familiar figure.

"Mrs. Van Rijt!" Jean exclaims, remembering. She was a family friend from Toronto days. She used to drive a silver Jaguar.

Mrs. Van Rijt, a shade plumper, gathers them affectionately into her arms, and Jean feels herself wrapping an arm around her waist – equals now. Being a good three inches taller she feels almost fatherly.

149

"You two look great, just great!" Mrs. Van Rijt exclaims. "Isn't this a super party!"

They are jostled by a large tan figure – Cody. He is juggling two drinks, coffee and a liqueur.

"Pardon me, fair ladies," he apologizes with an audible slur. Hot coffee splashes onto his wrist, and he scowls.

"You're bombed," remarks Colette.

"I am," he admits. "Purposefully and intentionally. And I am also rehearsing my speech." He pulls himself erect and sticks out his barrel chest.

"Rage, rage against the dying of the light!"

"Cody, you're not!" Jean pleads.

"Grave men, near death, who see with blinding sight . . ." he continues in a mellifluous brogue.

Colette looks disgusted. "Don't be an idiot, Cody."

There is a short hesitation as Cody stops his recital in mid-stanza. He nods once, then turns away, merging with the crowd of sweet-eaters. His pants are slipping, but with his hands full he can't tug them up.

"Who was *that*?" asks Mrs. Van Rijt.

"Friend of Dad's."

"Oh? I don't recognize him." She watches the retreating form, plainly puzzled, then plunges into another subject.

"The last time I saw you two girls was at the old house on Dundeen Square. Don't you remember, you were madly in love with that Japanese pianist, whatsisname?"

Jean supplies the name.

"Yes!" she prattles on. "There were pictures all over your room, and you used to pretend you were Japanese . . . We all wondered how long it would last. Do you ever see him? He's become very well known."

"Not since then," Jean says and eyes Colette. She's adopted a white mask, which betrays only mild irritation. "But he'll be in Vancouver tomorrow."

"Tomorrow!" cries Mrs. Van Rijt.

Jean regrets mentioning it.

"You'll be able to talk over old times!"

What a bizarre idea, Jean thinks. The notion of "talking over old times" with Yoshi, as if they were old school buddies, wingers on the hockey team.

"Irene Van Rijt!" Their father joins them, his hair tousled like a little boy's. He gives Irene a peck on the cheek.

"You look fabulous, Martin. A touch greyer, but it becomes you." Her voice has just shifted register, ringing a sultry contralto.

Unaccountably irritated, Jean grabs Colette's elbow and steers her away.

They stand under one of the poles that has been strung with lights.

"How are you doing?" Colette says.

"Okay," Jean snaps. "You?"

"All right. What I'd really like to do is split to the beach and stare at the moon."

Jean nods indifferently. "Did you realize that everyone in town knew about us – and him?"

"Maybe. Does it bother you?"

◻

We would let it drop, casually.

"Saturday? Oh, Yoshi Takahashi took us to see a movie: *Alice's Restaurant*. It was pretty good. And afterwards, we had supper at the Japan Gardens, and the waiter slipped rum into Yoshi's teacup."

Or, "Yoshi took us to Yorkville, to see Gordon Lightfoot play."

The three of us crowded into one side of a table. Colette on the outside sticking her legs into the aisle, Yoshi in the middle, and me pressed up against the wall.

We listened to Lightfoot do "Steel Rail Blues", so close to us we watched the sides of his mouth quiver on the held notes. It was smoky and it stung my eyes, but I was in my

151

first Yorkville coffee house listening to folk music. Yoshi had bought espresso, which we sipped cautiously, basking in its bitter taste.

"Well I got my mail late last night
A letter from the girl who found the time to write
To her lonesome boy
Somewhere's in the night."

Yoshi slung his arms over our shoulders and said, "This is the *real* music."

Afterwards, Lightfoot came over to our table with his guitar hooked behind his back and said, "I saw you sitting there, Mr. Takahashi. Hope you enjoyed the set."

"I like it very much," Yoshi said. "You have a very strong heart." He touched his own chest and let his hand rest there.

◻

"Do you still have your kimono, Colette?"

"Of course."

Jean wears hers every morning as she drinks her tea. It's light and fits loosely over her shoulders. And nowadays everyone in Manhattan is Japanese-crazy. For once Jean fits in.

"Do you wear it?"

"No, it's too small now, and raggedy." Colette flashes a smile. "But once a year I give it a careful wash in the sink and iron it. Come on. Let's go and get some coffee."

She gulps the last of her grapes while Jean deposits her still-laden plate on a table.

There is a sudden eruption of activity as the plate and contents scatter on the grass and Jean herself is nearly upended. A woman races by clutching her chest, her face stricken with fright.

"My heart's making a terrible sound!" she cries.

The man chasing her laughs and looks embarrassed.

□

He brought them back, a surprise, after a visit to his parents in Kyoto. I remember the way they looked in the box, identical blue cottons with silver thread mapping out the pattern of foliage. We tried them on over our clothes and he laughed at Colette, because it barely met her knees.

"I tell them in store these Canadian girls are very big!" he said, making a grand gesture with his arms. "But they don't make kimono so big. Now, you try *tabi* and *zōri* too."

The *tabi* were little white socks with a separate slot for the big toe. Colette didn't even want to try them and made excuses: "My feet are dirty." But I said, "Come on, Colette, don't be ashamed, just because your feet are so big." She flashed a dark look my way. But she had to then, and of course couldn't nearly get into the little socks; it was hard enough for me, and by the time we'd camped it up, making exaggerated grunting noises, Yoshi was in hysterics, rolling on the rug.

There was another box on the lacquered table: Colette noticed it too. The lid was half off, and we could see the brilliantly coloured cloth of another kimono, this one red silk.

"Who's this for?" I asked guilelessly.

For a moment, Yoshi was taken aback. "Oh, that is for friend of mine, she is singer, very beautiful singer."

Then he replaced the lid.

I forced an indifferent nod. We were just a tiny part of his life; comic relief perhaps.

□

There is a short line-up for Irish coffee: a splash of whisky, double-roasted brew, and—horrors—a squirt of whipped cream from an aerosol can.

"How did *that* get by Sam?" Jean whispers, accepting her portion gleefully.

The hot coffee and whisky knock through her system like a freight train.

"Colette?" Jean doesn't want her to go too far away.

Colette steps outside into the garden and Jean follows close by. The grass is trampled and wet. Several lights dot the pathway to the house while red lamps signal the portable toilets. Cody is emerging from one, fastening his fly while balancing his drink in the other hand. ZZZ – the bug zapper nabs another moth.

There's something Jean needs to find out. How can she ask without letting on she knows more? Colette's got to admit it on her own.

Jean presses a palm against a skinny tree. It's freshly planted and shifts under her weight.

"Colette?"

"Uh-huh." Colette sounds distracted.

"When we were lying in bed with him, with Yoshi, in Montreal . . . "

"Yes." Her voice is thin and impatient. "What about it?"

Jean sucks in a new breath. "And he was so careful to divide his attention equally – "

Colette turns, mocking. "You mean he made you come, then me, then you . . . "

Jean has to laugh, remembering the roller coaster, being kept at the peak so long she thought she'd faint from lack of oxygen.

"As I recall, when he turned to you, *he* came. Right? It was the only time."

"That's right, Jean." Oh, so patient. "Now, what is your question?"

"Only this: how did you do it?" Jean mimics Yoshi's accent. " 'Colette, you are very sexy girl!' "

That's what he said, a shot in the dark as Jean lay there on her back on the damp sheet.

"Colette — what exactly did you do to him?"

Colette wipes her mouth carefully with the back of her hand. She pauses and appears to think it over.

"What happened is simple," she says quietly. "He parted my legs and slipped it in. The whole thing didn't take more than ten seconds. Just parted my legs like a theatre curtain."

Slipped it in? It? Karate chop on the temple — No, a direct hit below the ribs. Where have I been? Jean wonders.

Parted my legs like a theatre curtain.

Take a deep breath and hold it forever. The years shoot off into space.

The whole thing didn't take more than ten seconds, she says.

One, two, three — what difference does it make? Why does it matter a goddamn if she did it first then, or the following year, or four years later? Why is this worse? Why is Jean's stomach heaving? Hand on the tree again.

It serves her right for asking.

Beside her, inches away. Without her. It was that instant, in that ten seconds that Jean lay in mind-numbing ignorance that she handed Colette over to him. A wind-up toy too busy listening to the yammering of her own heart.

I knew it all along, she thinks.

She races back toward the house, leaving Colette in startled silence under the tree, still hearing the dim resonance of her own words.

◻

The sight of Colette's rosy flesh pushing against the perfect lace of her bra and matching bikini underpants, while I strained to fill the saggy material of an undershirt, girls' department, Eaton's basement. That came from being a year younger. Underpants? I'd never thought of them till that moment when, standing in Fruit-of-the-Loom cotton "drawers" (that's the only word for them), I measured her, then me, and watched his almond eyes take in the whole of her bursting adolescence. I could have been a page boy, a newspaper vendor. I was sure he couldn't wait to get his hands on her, and I was right. With a delighted smile he captured both of us in his arms, one girl pushed to each side of his chest, and I saw out of the corner of my eye how fingers slipped under the material of her bra, his beautiful long piano fingers.

He tossed his blazer on the mattresses we'd spread on the floor. "I need a rest," he said, lying down. Would we like to join him, after taking a bath?

A bath? The two of us? Colette twisted the taps and sat on the porcelain ledge waiting for the tub to fill. I had no intention of taking off my underthings and exposing flesh to her critical stare. Instead we giggled and made exaggerated splashing noises so he couldn't fail to hear the tracks of cleanliness. We speculated nervously on what lay ahead and vowed to stay together. Promise till death, spoken on the precipice, Colette. The man was on the other side of the bathroom wall. She faced away, unhitched her bra (oh, that feminine gesture!), peeled off her panties and slipped a nightie over her head. It was a straightforward flannelette nightgown with eyelet embroidery at the yoke, probably a gift from Aunt Ruth, but the body underneath draped the material into unexpected curves.

I pulled a similar nightgown over my own head and watched its static drop to mid-calf.

We sneaked under the covers, one on either side of him. He was already asleep. And (we giggled on discovering this), he was naked! Neither of us had seen a naked man and didn't dare look for more than an instant. Suddenly there was a hint of danger.

He continued to sleep for a time as we lay politely staring at the ceiling. He had a concert to play, and we were mindful of this.

Suddenly a hand dropped lazily onto one thigh then another. We stiffened, lifted our heads, and exchanged glances. "Yes" was mirrored in each other's eyes. We waited, curious and expectant. Frozen in time. The hand danced up both thighs, girlish skin awakening under his touch. Yet we feigned sleep, or dream. What was *his* dream, Colette?

As the hand travelled, our legs fell open. Then he would have felt the difference. On one girl the womanish mound of hair, while the palm of the other hand slipped over a nearly naked fruit. He allowed his fingers to explore. Hard to keep his mind on both at the same time, the right hand doing melody, the left a thorough-bass.

I came first, with a nearly inaudible sound, but he sensed the opening up, then my legs squeezed around his fingers. He turned to the other with his magic hand and pressed until Colette came, too. By then, I was waiting impatiently, so he rolled back and nuzzled with his fingers, stroking differently this time, slower, so the rhythm would hunt out a new feeling. Whimpering, I fell back into the hot sheet.

Then. Only at the end did he recklessly push apart a pair of golden legs and press, blowing the warm liquid into the entryway at last.

Chapter Eleven

The studio is empty. Jean places her untouched glass of wine on the window ledge and sits down.

The cello lies on the floor in its case.

She snaps open the lid, lifts out the instrument with a practised heave, and jabs the endpin into the rubber disc.

His cello's bigger than Jean's – or so it seems. Smells different, too – almost sweet. She tightens the bow, which is so old the frog's worn into a little hollow where the fingers lie.

For the first time in weeks she plays without thinking, just lets her body pull the sound out till it fills the room with a crazy lament. To her amazement she is still breathing – deep exhalations between strokes, her lungs tugging at corners they haven't touched in months.

The song with no name spirals into the room, lassooing furniture, coiling into corners, and snapping back to meet the vibrating soundboard. Push and pull stretch into a continuum, her elbow a weightless anchor, the room an enlarged instrument she is inside of.

And when it is over it is because something has disturbed their song – a wave noisily cutting over the breakwater.

The door has opened. A dark shape enters and becomes Colette. Jean stops, realizes she is sweating, and lets the cello lean carelessly on her thigh.

Colette's face is composed yet pale.

"There's something we need to talk about," she says.

"I don't want to hear it." Leave me alone, Jean could say.

Colette looks around for a place to sit and chooses the window ledge. Without noticing, she knocks over Jean's glass of wine, which drips slowly onto the rug.

"There's something I haven't told you," Colette continues. Very quietly.

Resigned, Jean sinks into the chair.

"I've seen Yoshi since Montreal."

She waits for a reaction.

There is none, only the waiting.

"Months after Montreal," she continues, "he called me from New York to say he would be in Toronto and would I meet him at the Park Plaza roof garden." She eyes Jean carefully now, gauging her response. "I met him. He had a room there." She swallows. "He asked me to go with him to the room, and I did."

Jean's hand runs up and down the neck of the instrument, slippery and wet. A whirr of harmonics stirs from the strings like an insect.

"Are you okay?"

Jean nods.

Colette's voice resumes a more normal tone. "Then, I don't know, a year or so later he called from New York and invited me to visit. It was when you had moved there. He was very concerned that you shouldn't find out. He didn't want you to be hurt—"

Hurt. A stubbed toe, glass in the eye, stitches on a gashed forehead. I know about hurt, Jean thinks.

"That was the first time I stayed with you. It was so awkward. I hated the deceit and secretiveness, but what could I have done?" Colette's shoulders rise in challenge. "For a moment I thought it would be all right, that we were, I don't know, 'adult' enough to be honest. But I chickened out, it seemed to mean so much to you still . . . "

Jean can hear the music starting up outside again, signalling the return to the tables.

"I should have told you then, I think," Colette says.

"Why are you telling me now?" Jean whispers.

"Because you want to see him again. You keep insisting, and I try to put you off, and now you know why."

"Why not?"

"I don't understand."

"We should still see him, especially now."

"Oh no, Jean."

"I think so," Jean insists. "Don't you want to see what happens?"

Colette clamps her hands behind her head and sighs. "Why do you want to make it hard for yourself?"

Because I do, Jean thinks. I really do. I want to make us all sing at once.

Jean trails Colette back to the tent. Her fingers sting from pressing on strings after weeks of not playing. She realizes she's short of breath and stops for a moment, but it's not that, everything's speeded up. She's shaking like a puppy tossed out of a moving car.

Why do you want to make it hard for yourself? Colette asked.

Good question.

Jean's skin ripples from head to toe.

Maybe up close after all this time he won't be anything. Disappointing, like a favourite toy picked up in later life and discovered to be plastic. That would be best.

If only she believed it.

A distinctive blue van with orange lettering is parked on the flower bed outside the tent.

"What's the CBC doing here?" asks Colette.

A woman in a suit answers. "It's the *Journal*. Barbara Frum's going to interview Mr. Hopper."

"No kidding! Where is she? I'd like to meet her."

"In Toronto," the woman answers.

"Toronto?" Colette looks perplexed.

A passing crewman picks up an armload of cable and says, "Everything can be done from Toronto."

"Well." Colette sticks her hands on her hips. "Is that so?"

They take their places reluctantly, under the glare of television lights. Young men in jeans troop back and forth heaving heavy wires and camera equipment.

Martin stands up, shades his eyes, and calls into the audience.

"My dear friends," he begins.

The assembly gradually quiets down, though there are a few renegades.

"On with the party!" someone shouts. He is quickly hushed.

Martin bends forward, bouncing his thighs off the rim of the table.

"My wife has asked me to make an announcement of some interest — "

"Wait!"

All eyes fasten on a chubby figure awkwardly rising to his feet.

"Hang on, Cody." Martin tries to cut him off.

161

"No. I've come a long way."

"Tell that clown to sit down and shut up!" hisses Sam.

It's a stand-off. The two men stare at each other. At last Cody breaks into a grin, and simultaneously Martin sits down. The TV crew scrambles to shift the lighting.

"I *had* a speech." Cody holds up a crumpled wad of paper. "Rest assured it was just the thing you'd expect to hear from the best man at the Hopper wedding—"

"I *knew* I'd seen that fellow some place," stage whispers Uncle Charlie.

Cody tosses the clump of paper to the floor, then hitches up his trousers and begins to circulate through the tent.

"My speech had just the right balance of sentiment and nostalgia, anecdotes from the past, rash speculations for the future . . . "

Jean watches with fascination as the ball of paper slowly expands. There is nothing on it; it is completely blank.

"I was going to describe, for the second time in twenty-seven years, how these two met." Cody moves to a clear spot in front of the head table and stares directly at Sam and Martin.

"Sit down, Cody," says Sam wearily. She obviously doesn't expect him to obey.

Martin's arms are folded against his chest, and he stares at the tablecloth. He is trying to contain a smile that pries at the edge of his mouth.

Cody pivots toward the audience.

"I was going to relate to you how Martin and I were once buddies in New York City, living in the Village when it was still cheap. Beatniks, back when the word meant something. How I was skinny"—he sucks in his belly and smooths a hand over it—"skinny and wild-eyed and full of poetry . . . "

The student waiters have stopped circulating. They stand at the back of the tent and watch with obvious amusement.

The TV lights snap off, and the crew paces impatiently.

Sam sinks her face into her open palms. She peers through the splayed fingers like a prisoner.

Cody's voice gathers steam. "And how one day, a perfectly normal afternoon at Rienzi's on MacDougal Street, a remarkable beauty dropped into our midst. We didn't know what hit us – did we, Martin?"

Jean detects a slight nod; the merest bobbing of her father's head.

Colette's knee presses under the table.

"It was Samantha, a Canadian girl who sang or played harpsichord, or some damn thing."

"Cody," says Sam in an artificially gracious voice, "why don't you pour yourself a fresh drink and join our table?"

"Later." She is waved off. "My speech was full of that story – how, much to my amazement she chose *me*, at first. *Me*." Cody jams a finger against his chest. "With my one-room pad in a sixth-floor walkup, no hot water, grimy mattress on the floor, juice can full of butts, probably a copy of *Nausea* spread open on the floor."

Colette giggles.

"Who knows what might have happened had I not had that fatal human failing . . . " Cody pauses.

"Logorrhea," says Sam, tapping her knuckles on the tablecloth.

"Pride! I had to show her off. But as soon as she glimpsed Martin here it was all over for the Yank. I was no match for our friend: intense, talented, ambitious, refined – the jewel had found her ideal setting."

Martin begins to stir in his seat. He clears his throat as if preparing to speak.

Cody holds up a hand.

"In a minute, Martin, in a minute. She made a bee-line for you at that party in Barney Newman's loft, while you hung back, smoking those rancid Spanish cigarettes. One look at those elegant hands and she had to have you."

Cody walks briskly over to one of the side tables, lifts a half-empty wine bottle to his lips, and takes a long draught.

Sam winces.

"So," he continues, wiping his lips. "There was no duel. I loved Martin even more than I loved Samantha." An impish look crosses his face. "Besides, I still have his lovely daughters, don't I?"

Ha, ha. Jean tries to look as though she didn't hear that one.

Cody grins.

"But you'll all be glad to know that I've decided not to give that speech. Why speak of the past when we are plummeting into the future? Instead, let us sing what they sang on medieval feast days. A toast to our friends, Martin and Samantha Hopper!"

Another quick guzzle and Cody begins to sing, a raspy yet tuneful baritone:

"Who has good wine should flagon it out
And thrust the bad where the fungus sprout;
Then must merry companions shout:
THIS SONG WANTS DRINK!"

◻

"You girls have a wonderful time," Sam said, as we waited for notice of the train's arrival.

"We will."

Too excited for more than a perfunctory peck on the cheek, we left her waving under the Departures board. She was wearing that lime-green skirt that she had for years.

When we arrived in Montreal in mid-afternoon, clutching handbags and the plaid suitcase, a tall man marched up to us as we stood dazed on the train platform. "I'm

Ron, Yoshi's new manager," he said. "My car's outside."

His tone was curt, and almost immediately he turned his back. His European-tailored suit was a dark tweed, and the cuffs spread neatly over a pair of handmade boots.

We followed him obediently to the blue Volvo. How had he recognized us? we wondered.

Ron's only comment en route to the hotel was, "How long have you known Yoshi?"

"Five years!" we chorused. Sensing his disapproval we were trying not to giggle. Outside the window the city sparkled in late-fall clarity. We drove up to the Hotel Champlain, a century-old stone building. As we were about to step out of the car, Ron said, "No, stay here. I'm just depositing your suitcase. We'll drive straight to Symphony Hall for the rehearsal."

As he disappeared with our luggage Colette leaned over the front seat where she was sitting and said, "Do you think we're doing the right thing?"

"Of course we are," I said confidently. We couldn't let old Ron intimidate us. "He's only Yoshi's manager," I added.

"I guess you're right."

Ron returned, and we drove on through the strange and slightly exotic streets. I started out looking at every corner, every building, trying to lock it in memory, but soon the images became a flash flood and I gave up. It was better that way.

Symphony Hall was nothing like Massey Hall. The cement was new, the design practically space-age.

"Go through the side entrance and follow the hallway left," Ron instructed as we disembarked. Before we had a chance to thank him he'd sped off.

"How are you doing?" I said before opening the door.

Colette snatched my forearm. "Ex-*cited*."

I squeezed back.

As we entered the building we could hear the orchestral sound, random noises at first, but when we opened a second fire door it fell into a familiar cadence.

"Good old Beethoven Number Three," I grinned.

We stopped for a moment waiting for the piano entrance. There? A crystal sound. As always with Yoshi each note had a definite start and finish and you could almost see the little hammers working.

Did he remember we were coming? Perhaps he'd changed his mind. I swallowed over a mysterious bump in my throat.

"Should we go in?"

"Sure." Colette pointed toward the open door where the sound came from.

"Where does it lead to? What if it's direct to the stage?" I tried to hold Colette back. "Maybe Ron has tricked us on purpose."

"Don't be paranoid." She led the way through the door out into the hall.

Every seat was empty; we had our pick. Colette began to stroll toward the centre until I panicked.

"No! Let's sit at the side." I aimed circumspectly for an aisle seat behind a pillar. It was the old story again; we were to pretend that we weren't quite there, that we didn't know he would be there, that the whole thing was a bizarre coincidence. But this was different. Yoshi had invited us. It would be silly to hide when we were his guests. So I slid beside Colette into the second row, dead centre, and clasped my hands on my lap, breathing hard.

Yoshi, dressed in black sweatshirt and corduroys, sat at the piano directly above us. He crouched over, intent on a trill while the conductor, a Bernstein look-alike, watched, hands on hips. The concert-master wiped his nose with his bow hand.

It was a perfect trill.

Suddenly there was a sound from the back ranks of the orchestra. A portly woman stood up, French horn tucked under arm, and called, "Time, Maestro."

166

Yoshi looked up, played a few bars of silent movie music ending with a dissonant chord, and rose to his feet. The conductor slipped his baton into a little sheath on the podium and said, "Twenty minutes, ladies and gentlemen."

The orchestra members immediately began to disassemble, leaning instruments against chairs, slipping them into cases or onto special stands.

Colette leaned her mouth near my ear and whispered a play-by-play of the scene: "He scratches his head; he puts one foot up on the bench; he yawns . . . " As if I couldn't see for myself.

We watched Yoshi confer with the conductor, the two of them hunched over the giant score. Yoshi sang out the line in a hoarse "da-da-da" and conducted, with one hand, an imaginary orchestra. The Bernstein clone nodded several times, tapping his fingers against his teeth.

Suddenly we were discovered.

"Co-lette! Jean!" He waved. He smiled. We waved and smiled back, rising from our chairs into the air.

"You wait," he said and, after a few more words with the conductor, he did a handspring off the stage and suddenly he was there, that miracle face propped on the back of the seat in front of us.

"So," he said, simultaneously shaking a hand of each of us. "You are here. You made it."

"We made it, Yoshi."

"How does orchestra sound?" he asked.

"Good." We bobbed up and down.

"What about acoustic?" he frowned. "I'm not so sure they are good for me here. Can you hear everything?"

He was asking us! Suddenly we became serious, thoughtful even. I wrinkled my brow and said tentatively, "To tell the truth, the brass section could use a little clarity. I could see them blowing hard, but it sounds murky."

What nerve! I hoped I was right.

He nodded. "The hall is not good for brass balance. They say they fix it—" He pointed up at huge levels of baffles above the stage. "But it is still not so good. What about piano? Can you hear piano?"

"Oh, yes," we chimed. "The piano is clear as day."

Laughing he reached over and messed our hair. "You girls are very good for ego. Maybe I take you with me everywhere."

I sucked air; dared we hope . . . ? A picture formed of a life accompanying Yoshi, of camping with him in hotel rooms across the world, of rehearsals with the Vienna Philharmonic, the Berlin Philharmonic, the Amsterdam Concertgebouw, of Von Karajan for lunch, of jetting to Tokyo and Amsterdam, of rubbing his tight shoulders after concerts . . .

"Did Ron take care of you?" he asked.

"Sort of," Colette said.

"Oh?" Yoshi cocked his head. "Sort of. What do you mean?"

"Ron took care of us," I said quickly. "He put our suitcase in the hotel."

"Good," he said. "I have to go back to work now. Is this okay for you? Are you bored?"

"No, no!" we cried. Bored??

"You don't have to stay here. You can look around and meet me later for dinner. I be through" — he consulted the clock on the back wall — "in one hour."

"It's okay," we said. "We want to stay and watch."

That night we sat in our box seats and watched Yoshi play the concerto. Afterwards the audience rose as one to give him a standing ovation. A young woman carried a dozen roses onstage and handed them to him. He bowed once, then motioned the orchestra to rise, but they stayed seated, tapping their stands with bows and fingertips. Smiling, the conductor leaned against the railing of his podium and watched.

We cheered, and "bravos" sailed through the air like confetti. Yoshi, our friend! Pride swelled up in my chest

168

till I thought I'd burst, but instead I cried "Bravo" and Colette glanced at me, surprised.

"Bravo!" The sound shot through my arms and legs, opening every pore. I was the last one to shout it into the dizzy hall.

Afterwards, backstage, he stood in his black kimono, drenched in sweat. Tactfully we stood in the background, easy now in our friendship. A line-up of people clutching programs waited to see him.

"*Extraordinaire!*" someone exclaimed. "*Il est un vrai maître!*"

A woman of about Sam's age, wearing a canary-yellow suit, pushed through and practically attacked Yoshi with enthusiasm. She pumped his hand, then began to tell him, in a confidential tone that reached every corner of the room, about her genius of a daughter.

"Amy is taking her Master's degree in piano at the Curtis with Fritz Holder," she declared. "You must know him!"

I flinched with distaste.

But Yoshi nodded, even as the woman proceeded to repeat Amy's name at least three times, tapping Yoshi's shoulder for emphasis. When he returned the program, signed and dedicated to the soon-to-be-famous daughter, he smiled and took her hand again.

As the woman swooped past us she sang euphorically, "Isn't he wonderful!"

At last people began to clear out. The manager of the hall lingered, and Yoshi picked up several heaps of flowers and pressed them on him.

"You take these home for wife; they only die in hotel room."

As he closed the door behind the manager, Yoshi's face suddenly changed, like a tent with its pole kicked out.

"Now I relax!" he declared, then swooped us into a hug. We danced with him in a little circle on the floor. Then he let go and looked at us intently.

"How you feel?"

We gave uncertain smiles.

With quick understanding he said, "This is crazy life. I get dressed, then we have supper with conductor and some music people. You like seafood?"

"Sure," we said, wondering how the music people would like us.

Yoshi changed into street clothes while sitting on the floor, first slipping a pair of black jeans under the kimono. Then taking off the robe he reached, bare chested, for a worn green sweatshirt with a decal reading: "MARLBORO FESTIVAL '70".

In it he looked maybe twenty years old.

"So, we are ready, all dressed and clean. Is my face on?" He leapt to his feet and mugged for us.

He was our Yoshi again, and we laughed happily, the three of us loping arm in arm through long cement corridors toward the crisp Montreal evening. A familiar car waited, the Volvo driven by Ron, who was suddenly gracious, opening doors and making pleasant conversation about the concert and the supper to come.

At Le Continental twenty of us sat at a long table and peered at the menu. It looked expensive.

"You have anything you want: lobster, scallop ... " Yoshi whispered.

We were surrounded by the cream of Montreal musical life, all yearning for a word with Yoshi.

"Yoshi, where are you going next? Do you plan to be in Paris next month for the Debussy Festival?"

"Yoshi, remember the time we went to that wonderful sushi bar in Tokyo ... ?"

"Yoshi, do you know that old friend of ours in Florence ... ?"

Most of the time I couldn't speak. I picked at the food without tasting a bite. After a time a long-haired tympanist leaned toward us and said with a wry smile, "So, you're in the inner circle."

170

I blushed. But Colette looked delighted and replied, "We've known him since he came to Toronto!"

"Have you now!" The percussionist nodded, still smiling. He wore handpainted ceramic beads around his neck and an Indian shirt with little mirrors sewn on. Nobody else said a word to us, except Yoshi. From time to time he hid his face from the rest and let us see his exhaustion, his eyes rolling and his mouth turned way down at the corners.

For dessert we drank cognac – again. As I lifted the flowerpot-sized snifter to my lips, Yoshi leaned over and said gently, "You remember cognac?"

"Of course."

I remember it all.

Chapter Twelve

Martin sticks two fingers in his mouth and whistles. This is so out of character that everyone stops gabbing.

"The first thing I would like to announce," he begins, "is the presence of our esteemed architect, Derek Arthur." Making a visor out of his hand he scans the crowd.

A small, compact man stands and bows to strenuous applause.

Sam's face radiates pride as she raises her hands above her head.

"Naturally, it's been twice as expensive as forecast," Martin continues.

Mr. Arthur looks pained.

"But what's money when you've got symmetry and beauty!"

More appreciative applause.

"Announcement number two." He raises his glass and practises tipping it in various directions without spilling the contents.

The TV lights are switched on again, and a camera swings in tight. We stare at the speaker, our chins tilted, wearing expressions of curiosity and expectancy.

"Announcement two may seem rather confusing in light of announcement one," he concedes. "The fact is, we never really expected announcement two to transpire, but then I always underestimate the determination of my wife."

Sam smoothes the sleeves of her dress and beams blindly into the audience.

"We have been invited, starting in September, to direct the School of Western Classical Music in" – he pauses, swallows, then pronounces impeccably – "Be-jing!"

A collective gasp.

Stunned, Jean stares at Colette, who stares back open-mouthed.

The wave of applause begins at the back tables and spreads until everyone is standing, except Sam.

Jean claps frantically, palms slapping like a manic tortilla maker, trying to hear herself above the others.

"Okay, okay." Martin is waving his arms in the air. A crescent-shaped sweat mark glistens under his sleeves.

Jean finds her seat and perches rigidly.

"Of course," – his voice unsuccessfully masks excitement – "this has been a co-operative venture. I would like to introduce the prime movers, Mr. Erskine of the Department of External Affairs . . . "

There is a shuffle, and a slim, blond man threads his way through the tables to the front.

Jean watches with astonishment, then twists so she can see Colette, whose surprised gaze collides with her own.

It's the young man in the olive suit Colette was chatting with earlier.

Did she know about this all along? Is that what they were speaking of so furtively?

No, plainly she's as astonished as Jean.

"And from Mainland China, I would like very much to introduce our major sponsor, Doctor Chou Lin Yueng!"

A second figure, in a boxy suit and heavy glasses, presses to the front. The waiting microphone is a bulbous knob decorated with a CBC emblem.

"Thank you very much," Dr. Chou begins, as a second wave of applause fills the tent.

"On behalf of my government I am very pleased to invite Dr. Martin Hopper and his wife, Samantha, to direct, for a period of three years, the Bejing School of Western Classical Music . . . "

Sam and Martin start to shimmer and drift at the edges as though torn from a wedge of impossibly sheer silk.

The Chinese man continues to speak in a stiff accent, occasionally referring to a page of notes. The table shakes like crazy – someone's knee popping its underside.

"What do you think of all this, hon?" Sam's arm swings over Jean's shoulder. "Did you *ever* guess?" she whispers.

Jean can only shake her head. The weight of Sam's arm is reassuring.

The speeches continue.

It's terrifically hot and humid in the tent. The blasting heat from the arc lamps makes Jean's skin prickle. She sees that Colette has propped her head in her hands.

Bejing? The map in her mind undulates, refusing to locate this sound. China is a vague frozen land mass – over there. Purple and covered in mountains.

Think of something cool, something lean and peaceful: The shaved head of the *shakuhachi* player bows. He presses the long flute to his lips, then overblows the mouthpiece, shaking his head from side to side, the sound rising and falling with his long breath. It is the sound of wind shaking through a grove of decaying bamboo trees . . .

"Congratulations!" someone shouts, and it begins again, the clapping. Jean joins in, feeling a nest of crows in her throat.

"Let the band play!"

There is a chaotic movement as chairs and tables are pushed to the sides. A trumpet bleats experimentally through a screeching mike. Within moments the centre of the tent is cleared, the ground littered with chunks of wilted lettuce.

Sam and Martin disappear inside for the Barbara Frum interview. The CBC crew follows. Jean watches their purposeful stride.

"Let the band play!"

And it does, an up-tempo "Big Noise From Winnetka", and Jean can't help it, her toes start jiggling inside her slingbacks.

"I know this song!" she says aloud and looks around for a response.

"Step out?" Cody asks, and performs an oddly graceful pirouette.

They find an empty spot near the dessert table where he expects Jean to jive. She doesn't know how, but she wants to dance fast, cut the rug like an upended chainsaw.

"You knew all about this," she accuses, letting herself whip into his stomach.

"Your dad wrote me."

She swings out again on the edge of her heels.

"Really?"

"Really. Mad?"

She's being twirled like a top—too dizzy to respond.

"I don't think he wants to go," adds Cody.

"Why not?" She freezes, attentive.

"For one thing, he hates flying."

"Oh . . . well." She walks under his raised arm and they get into a snarl. Unwinding, they end up back to back with Cody talking over his shoulder.

"And another thing—ever since he's been invited, the

government's been nosing around his past. Found out he was a member of the CP once."

"Dad, a Communist?"

"For five minutes, back in the fifties. And he signed some mildly radical faculty petitions."

"Really?" Jean lets herself bat against Cody's shoulderblades. "I never thought of him as the least bit radical."

"Shocked?"

"Hardly," Jean scoffs. She remembers the Mountie's phone call. Colette will be amused.

"Of course," continues Cody, "Sam choreographed this whole adventure. She made the connections with the embassies. Martin's scared out of his tree."

"Scared? Of what?"

"You should know. Of . . . weird food, not speaking the language, not being in control."

Thank God Cody's given up the jive, and they perform a rocking dance, shadow-boxing nearly.

"Why do you think he's chosen the life he has, instead of busting into the world of solo artists . . .?"

"Dad? He's not good enough." The words come easily.

"Bullshit! He's got the chops but not the spots!"

"Mmm?"

His face moves in, wide and red-veined.

"He doesn't have the hide for it, he's a forest creature who shrinks from bright lights. Make no mistake, Martin's as good as anyone, but he made a choice way back before he knew it. Poor Sam, didn't realize she'd married a *real* artist, not a show-biz shaman."

You've got it wrong, Jean wants to say. Father needs the push, would fall into the sea without it. Same as she'd be devastated if he actually sailed off, spinnaker taut, before the wind.

"He's not a coward."

"Never said he was."

As Cody sweeps her through the throng, Jean holds on tight, resting her chin on his shoulder.

"There she is!"

"Who?" he asks.

"Colette. She's leaning against the tent post, watching us."

"Relax." Jean feels his hand pressed against her hipbone.

"I just want to make sure she has a good time." This sounds false even to Jean.

"Jean," he says, close as a bug in her ear. "Don't you think it's about time you left home?"

Her dad sails by with Sam in his arms. Both are laughing, Sam in a trickling glissando.

Suddenly Jean feels blazed with power. In a day she'll be back in New York, and none of this will matter. None of it. If Colette chooses to sneak a weekend with Him, Jean needn't know. The city's plenty big enough for all of them — big as China.

Cody stops, mid-beat.

"You leading, or me?"

"I am."

"Suit yourself. Long's I know."

Jean leads them through the bumping couples till they're jammed in the heart of it, right up near the band. Cody winces.

"Why so close?"

It's where Jean saw them, hunched in the shadow of Max Romeo's cough, the arc of his microphone missing their heads by inches.

She's so strong she could lift a cannon, run for Prime Minister.

"You're a good dancer," she says instead.

"Bullshit!"

The flesh moves under her hands in circles, and she feels him pulling away from her. Why? She presses in as the sax

177

performs a dumb solo, with faked intensity, but Cody drops his arms and stands back a step.

"What's up?" Jean shouts.

"I'm too hot."

"Then let's scoot!" She propels him through the crowd again.

"Maybe you better calm down," he's saying as they continue their close-limbed dance in the dark, outside.

"Like hell I will."

But her eyes fill with tears. Why, she's not sure.

"Hey," he whispers, rubbing her shoulder gently. His groin scoops into hers, and she presses back, for balance.

A few yards away the band stops to tune, and it sounds as though the bass guitar has broken a string. The musician winds up, plucking hard as he twists the peg, and the note screams higher, like a train coming into the station. What's that called? Her brain scrambles a moment. The Doppler effect.

"The last time I danced," she says, sucking the tears back, "was at the big library benefit."

"I was there."

They part and look at each other. "That's incredible, you must figure in my destiny," she declares. There's an artificial lilt to her voice.

"I guess so." With the light behind him she can see every bit of the edge of his face, each bristle. She's fascinated by his naked scalp, that private skin now glistening sweat.

Then she remembers.

"Is it true, about you and Sam?"

He lights up a cigarette and exhales slowly, still rocking from side to side. They watch the rings halo over his head.

"It's true what I said. I was crazy about her."

"Are you still?" Just a guess.

He doesn't answer. Jean tries to imagine it: Sam with a past. The New York she's read about and tried to find, hunting down old bars and finding them dead, or filled with people like herself. It's gone. Sam beat her to it.

She almost laughs aloud. No wonder Sam can't stand to see him now, to be reminded. His slim beatnik body buried forever.

Cody flicks the cigarette to the ground where it smoulders. The guitar, after its brief, squealing crescendo, has settled into a plodding bass line. Thump-thumpa-thump, only there if you listen hard.

"Did you—"

"She was so young, much smaller, yet proud as all get-out—"

"Did you—" Jean tries again, cheeks sucked in, savouring a sour taste in her mouth. "Did you and Colette make love last night?"

There is a stunned silence. His eyebrows shoot up into his forehead and hover there, waiting.

"What?"

Jean plows on, repeating the question.

"You're crazy, Jean."

"Did you?" Like a child. Did you? Did you?

"When?" He throws his hands into the air, baffled. "Don't you remember, we got hammered, the three of us, on the beach. You two had to dump me in bed. I was in no condition for anything."

"You're not answering."

He's annoyed, and she's afraid he won't reply, on principle. It's her tone: she should have made a joke of it. Another couple passes nearby, sees them, then scuttles off in another direction.

"Of course not," he says. "Do you want us to have fucked? Would it make you angry enough?" He adds aggressively, "Angry enough to want to get back at her?"

It's beginning to rain. Just enough so the few people outside the tent move back in. Jean likes the cool feel of water on her face. Cody glances back toward the tent but doesn't budge.

"Let's go!" She grabs his hand and heads toward the bright green Johnny-on-the-Spot.

Pushing the door open they plunge inside, just in time, as the sky opens and the rain rattles down on the tiny roof. A dim light hangs above as they cram up against each other. She sets a foot on the toilet-seat rim, since it won't fit anywhere else, and they bob around inside the shed, rocking it.

"I feel like a ship in a bottle," Jean says.

Cody wrinkles his nose. "What do they use for disinfectant?"

"Shhh." She presses a finger on his lips. Up close, his face is huge and flat.

His arms swell around her and hers around him. She thinks of him slim, with a neat beard and black turtleneck. Reaching up she runs a hand over his ear and around to the back of his head. The skin is taut and smooth and slightly damp.

He loses his balance and tips back against the wall so the structure rocks alarmingly. Jean steels herself for a fall, but it doesn't happen. Still, with one foot she flips the toilet lid shut – just in case.

There's a crash of thunder, a moment of breathless anticipation, then the light goes out with a sizzle.

At first there is nothing. Then the two of them, Cody and Jean, his face moving against hers, the beard stripping her skin like some marauding bear. He unbuttons her silk blouse, and it slips off her shoulders onto the floor, to be unavoidably trampled. She mourns for less than a second. The zipper on her skirt lowers smoothly and unwraps her hips. She reaches down and struggles with his buckle until it springs open. He waits then, arms at sides, as she pulls his trousers down. Everything is alive, even the cloth. All by touch, as she can't see a thing, not even eyes glowing in the dark. He burrows his head between her breasts while

180

she wraps her legs around his, squeezing hard, singing into the rain.

If you could see us now, Colette.

His face slips down her belly button, between her legs, and then a wet tongue enters her insides, spinning nimbly as an acrobat.

She doesn't know if he feels it happening, but she does, and she doesn't care. As they dive into the back of the shed, the thing tips up on two legs, bucking, and teeters there a split-second before crashing sideways into the wet turf. Somewhere below, Cody's head is manacled between her legs and he bellows in alarm.

Then laughter, fast and explosive, two monks suddenly reaching enlightenment.

The fibreglass coffin bends in. She worries about the toilet, expecting to feel the splash over her belly any moment.

"Jean?"

"Uh?"

"It's fallen on top of its door; we can't get out."

"Can't get out . . . " she repeats, and rides another wave of hysteria.

He shifts position, and her elbow falls through free space and hits something soft – her blouse, her poor wrecked silk.

◻

"Can I kiss you down there?" asked Yoshi. His mouth was pressed into the whiteness of my belly.

"No!"

I refused before imagining it, knowing only that it had never happened before. I don't want him so far away, I told myself. I didn't know anything.

His mouth rose to my shoulder – then Colette's. He never once kissed us on the lips – did he? Later, did Colette find them wet? – or dry as the finest rice paper?

181

"I can't stand this," grunts Cody. "It's claustrophobic."

"How are we going to escape?"

"We'll have to rock it. Hold tight."

They grasp each other till they form a single unit.

"One, two, three, *rock*!" They lunge toward the other side of the container.

A catastrophe. Cody thrusts against the corner while Jean somehow slips away, counter-balancing. Naturally his greater weight tips the box, and they hang like a safe over a ledge.

"Wait, Cody!" she squeaks. "Which way is up?"

"God damn it, Jean, get over here!"

Tentatively, she reaches for his hand then slides down until over they go, a chaotic somersault ending with the door springing open and the welcome stain of rain.

Chapter Thirteen

"Good sleeping," yawns a voice from the blackness of the bedroom. Jean feels around for the sleeping bag. She hoped Colette would be asleep.

"Still want to go to the mainland tomorrow?" the voice continues.

"Yes." Jean tosses her muddy clothes onto the floor and slips naked into the bag.

"You're nuts."

"Maybe."

"You're not," the voice falters, "planning to do something silly?"

"I haven't decided yet."

"Does it occur to you" – Colette shifts position and rests her chin on her hands – "that this will be tougher on me than you?"

Jean is deliberately silent. Her head is racing with liquor. When she shuts her eyes she is still falling.

"I haven't seen him in months," pleads Colette. "We decided it was over."

"Months?" Why this lie, now? "That's not true, Colette." A silence.

"What do you mean?"

"It was my birthday." Jean zips the bag up her side, closing herself in tight. She assumes a disembodied, story-telling voice.

"A bright spring evening when my friend Reuben and I left the theatre. If I had my choice, he asked, where would I go next? CBGB's I said."

Jean hears a soft sigh, like a cat stirring from a dream.

"Yes, June the seventh," she continues. "A gorgeous evening, not too hot yet, the city still on its toes. The world was my oyster, my oyster."

There is still music jangling outside in the tent, or is it in her head now?

There is no response across the room. Perhaps Colette has fallen asleep.

"When we opened the door," she recalls, "my eyes burned from the cigarette smoke. The joint was jammed. Max Romeo and theWild Sins of Mexico. Isn't that a crazy name for a band?" She cocks her head. "Imagine my surprise when I spied, lurking in the front like . . . like a couple of hit men, the unmistakable profiles . . . "

"All right, Jean. Cut it. That's enough."

So she's awake. Good. Jean plows on in the same arti-ficial, sing-song voice.

"At first I thought the smoke was playing tricks on me. Sort of a dry-ice attack. But I squinted and looked again and sure enough . . . "

"What do you want me to say, Jean? I'm sorry?"

Jean pauses to consider. "I want you to know just how I felt. Feel the same cut across the rib cage. Don't get too

184

comfortable lying there. Imagine yourself walking across the street in a pleasant daze, maybe thinking of a movie or a song, and all of a sudden you look up and see this Mack truck bearing down on you, all bumper and flashing lights and—"

"Listen to me!" Colette raps the oak floor. "Sure, you're mad and hurt—I don't mind that. But don't rant on like this. Your little speech. How long have you been prowling around with it, waiting for the right moment? No wonder you're so weird this weekend, stalking me like—like a hit man. If you want to talk, talk to *me*. I'm still the same person."

Equally sharp, Jean says, "Why did you just say you hadn't seen him in months, that you'd decided it was over?"

Colette sighs painfully. "I didn't want to make it even harder."

"For you, you mean. How patronizing!" Jean spits the word.

"Stop it!" Colette is breathing hard. "I did nothing wrong. I didn't do anything you wouldn't have done if you were given the chance—if he'd chosen you."

Jean's eyes are adjusting to the darkness. Above, the ceiling begins to take on texture, a mottled surface. She feels, for a moment, as if she were pinned in a space capsule, staring at the moon.

"Why was it you?" she asks softly.

There is an uncomfortable laugh. "I guess he sensed I'd moved beyond the threesome. It's got nothing to do with not liking you, Jean. He often speaks of you fondly, asks what you're up to. He would have liked for all of us to get together in New York, but it was too dangerous. You would have guessed, and he knew that would be too hard. You weren't ready."

Jean presses her palms over her temples and squeezes until a sharp pain races down her spine.

"Why don't you deny everything!" she cries. "If you

really cared for me that's what you'd do. Say it couldn't have been you that night, on my birthday. My birthday, for God's sake!"

Suddenly the darkness is shattered by a flood of intense light. What's going on? Her hands spring from her temples. What's she done to herself?

Colette, all naked pale skin, is bent over, leaning her impossibly large face in close to Jean's. Another six inches and their noses would touch.

Instinctively, Jean stiffens, forcing herself not to blink into the light.

The lips move. The hands tuck under Jean's shoulders and begin to shake them.

"Wake up, Jean. You don't mean that! We're not going to bullshit any more!"

Shake, shake, shake, till her teeth chatter.

The room swims a few strokes then stops for breath.

"Please – stop – shaking – me!"

Just as suddenly Colette lets go and drops to a crouch beside the sleeping bag. She slides her legs up and sinks her chin onto her knees. The fluorescent lights buzz and whirr, casting a shadowless glow over her skin. She's all goose-pimply. Her breasts fall into the middle of the triangle her body makes.

Funny, thinks Jean, I forget she has breasts.

"I –" she begins, then stops. There's nowhere to go.

"Shhh," whispers Colette.

The sound whistles straight through her ears.

She's shivering, thinks Jean. I could ask her to slip into bed with me; like summers at the cottage when we were afraid of the dark. She would come, I'm sure she would. She's waiting for me.

"I tried to talk you out of meeting him tomorrow." Colette is rocking back and forth. "I couldn't wait and let you find out then. That would have been really cruel."

After a moment she adds, "I wasn't lying when I said

it's over now. That was our last time together. I had to do it. It had dragged on too long. I was always waiting for the next time Yoshi would call, bid me to come. Nelson must have felt it. It couldn't go on forever."

She clasps her knees and says eagerly, "I just wish I could have told you from the beginning. You're the only person in the whole world who . . . "

"All together, how often?"

"What?"

"How often did you see him, alone?"

Colette considers. "Seven or eight times, over the years."

"That's not much."

"No," Colette breathes. "Not much at all."

Jean twists her head on the pillow and meets Colette's eyes.

"It must have been something," she says.

"Yes. It was something."

Chapter Fourteen

The microchip watch chirps the wake-up song at 9:00 A.M. Not that Jean slept more than a moment. Light pours into the bedroom, and a gust of morning ocean air cuts through the haze of stale cigarette smoke.

Jean inhales deeply. Something invisible presses down on her scalp, filling her head with the tumble of ball bearings.

"It's time," she whispers to the prone figure on the floor.

Colette's face is lost in the pillow.

Jean is tempted. She could slide cozily back into the bag, batten shut her eyes for another three hours, and it would be over.

"I'm coming," mumbles a muffled voice. Colette yawns loudly and stretches her arms into the air. A vein flexes in her forearm.

Too late now.

Jean heads for the bathroom, peering into the living-room on the way at the sprawl of bodies on cots, sofas, the floor. One bulky shape is perched on the lip of the conversation pit breathing loosely like a resonating drum head.

She won't wake him. He'll be gone before her return. She has a dim memory of an arrangement made: some bar they are to meet in on a specific date. She's forgotten which one and which date. She stands a moment, undecided, watching the big shoulders rise and fall under the sheet. The room is thick with cigarette smoke, the scent of roses, and it's hard to breathe. She continues to tiptoe over the oak floor down the hallway. Her lips are cracked and her teeth probably stained red from wine. If he likes, he can leave her a note.

The bathroom door is tipped open, and there's a sound of gargling. It stops.

"That you, Colette?"

"No, it's me."

"Come on in." Sam spits into the sink. She's wearing her husband's flannel dressing-gown with braided collar and cuffs.

"I can wait."

Sam watches her in the mirror. "Come on in and shut the door."

Jean, too weak to argue, obeys. She perches on the rim of the bathtub. The room is steamy.

"Have a good time?"

"Sure."

"You don't sound sure."

"I'm a little hung over."

"Aren't we all. It *was* a good party, wasn't it?"

Sam recaps the mouthwash and scowls at her reflection, then turns so she's facing her daughter.

"You haven't said anything about our surprise announcement. Once the dancing started you disappeared somewhere – with Cody Sayles." She doesn't bother masking her disapproval.

"It got hot inside the tent."

Sam searches her daughter's eyes.

"You're not going to see that man again?"

"Why should I?" says Jean casually. "New York's a big place."

After a brief pause, Sam returns to her normal voice.

"What do you think? Isn't it thrilling about China? Think I'll look good in a Mao jacket?" She poses, hand on jutted hip.

"You'll look terrific, Mom. It's an incredible opportunity. I can hardly believe it."

"Me neither," giggles Sam. "We're going to language classes three times a week. Listen."

She tilts her chin and says something incomprehensible, queer sing-songs from her throat.

"Wow," says Jean, impressed. "You sound really Chinese."

"Thanks. It means, 'Please speak more slowly.' Remember that other business, Jean? Is there anything I can do to persuade you to come and stay in the new house? At least try it for a year? What are we going to do about poor old Ace? We can't take him with us, and I'd hate to have to put him down."

"You wouldn't!" Jean clutches the edge of the bathtub.

"What do you suggest?" Sam blinks anxiously at her daughter. "You don't look so hot yourself." She reaches into the medicine cabinet and pulls out a vial of aspirin. "Here, take a couple of these."

Jean holds out her hand.

"You girls going to the mainland today?"

"That's the plan." Jean swallows the pills noisily, without water.

"Do you want me to fix you some breakfast?"

"No, no, we're going out."

"Don't blame you." Sam yanks a clump of hair out of her brush and drops it in the toilet. "Looks like I'll be hostess for a while yet. Before you disappear, drop by our bedroom to say goodbye. I want to take a look at you."

"Okay."

"I'll leave you to it." Then Sam makes a sound. "That's 'See you later' in Cantonese," she says.

Jean closes the door gently behind her mother. She twists the hot-water faucet on full blast and fills the room with a fresh cloud of steam.

Colette is already dressed and standing in the middle of the room dangling a leather bag. She's wearing a bright-red paratrooper's suit with a blue scarf knotted around her waist.

"Parade gear," she says, with a hint of apology.

Or combat, thinks Jean. "My clothes are so dull," she says and picks through the suitcase, finally settling on a pair of dark corduroys and a V-neck summer sweater.

She dresses quickly then stares into the mirror and runs a knob of lipstick over her mouth. "Nervous?"

Her eyes are raccoon-rimmed and too small.

"A little," admits Colette. "I don't know why we're doing this."

"Neither do I," says Jean brightly. "But look at us — we are."

The mood aboard the ferry is sombre, as if they're travelling to visit a dying relative. Jean pretends to read magazines, then leans against the deck railing and lets the wind sift through her hair.

A fishing boat passes a hundred yards away, a blue and white cap bobbing in the wake of the larger vessel.

◻

He fished out a key and twisted the lock. Still we didn't know for certain. The door sprang open, and we saw his stuff there – a leather bag on the bed, a shirt draped casually over the chair – and the TV set left on.

Our bag stood just inside the door, bold as can be.

"Yoshi," Colette said with soft amusement, "you told our parents we would have our own suite."

He walked abruptly toward the phone.

"I call the front desk for another room." Perched on the bed he began to dial.

"*Colette*," I hissed. "Fix it!"

She reached over and touched his wrist. "It's okay, I was just kidding."

"You sure?" he paused, finger in the slot. "I can get you another room if you're not comfortable."

Colette looked at me. "We're comfortable."

What a delicious lie!

"So." He sighed and fell back against the headboard. "Here we are."

"Here we are," we giggled. My head swirled with it. I held onto the bedpost and waited for the room to shape up. We were blessed, Colette, we were being handed the fantasy we'd never dared dream of, and the air was thin. Outside, sirens howled and we later found out a landmark church was burning down.

□

The record store is downtown on the Granville Mall next to a take-out frozen-yogurt joint. The street is crowded with people watching each other. A street musician plays slide trombone, not too well, and collects money – in a violin case.

"Figure that one out," says Colette.

They are panhandled twice, and comply both times.

Plastered to the store window is a blowup of Yoshi's face, each pore enlarged, the smile a six-foot-wide chasm.

A sign reads: "Internationally renowned pianist YOSHI TAKAHASHI signs copies of his new digitally recorded LP from Deutsche Grammophon: Eric Satie: *Nocturnes.* 2:00-3:00 P.M."

"We've got the right day," breathes Jean. "Pass me your comb."

At first they don't see him in the assembly of well-dressed fans, mostly female, clutching the distinctive yellow-bannered records. Finally Colette whispers, "There!" and sure enough they spy him sitting behind a cafeteria-style table, blinking back flashbulbs with a familiar smile. Jean turns away abruptly. The light is dazzling. They could stay there a moment, watching, and leave before he notices. It would be enough.

"He looks how he always did," she whispers. "Hasn't aged an inch."

"I know," says Colette. She too is staring.

Jean snatches a record off the display, despite the fact that she hasn't a stereo in New York. The cover has a close-up of his face. The colour of betrayal is red and black and yellow.

The line draws closer. A television camera is trained on him, and for a moment that smile is floodlit, creating dazzling after-images.

"We could leave," Jean says. But it's too late; they are caught in it.

Yoshi looks up, squints, and sees them. His mouth drops.

"I don't believe it!" he cries, rising to his feet. The camera follows.

They press to the foreground, the crowd springing open like a hand. He reaches across the table and gives them a tight hug, rocking them. His cheek is perfectly smooth and slightly damp from the lights.

She is close enough to his ear to whisper something, shoot a poisoned dart right through the drum. He wouldn't know what hit him.

"I was thinking of you girls a couple of days ago," he declares. "I was in Montreal at the Hotel Champlain. You remember Montreal?"

"Of course!"

His eyes rest on both of them, equally. "You live here now?"

"No," Colette answers. "We're visiting our parents."

"Family is living here?"

"That's right."

What a faker. It's as if . . . Jean hardly dares think. Perhaps she didn't see them in the bar at all. The lights were low, and the smoke dense. She sways uneasily, fingering the record. Colette stands stock still beside her, hands plunged deep into the pockets of her jumpsuit.

Yoshi turns to the group of men hovering nearby.

"You must meet my very old friends from Toronto," he says. "This is Nicky, my manager."

A young man dressed in a crisp summer suit nods.

"And Stan, record company man."

Another polite nod.

"Krakoff, from Vancouver Symphony."

Smiles and outstretched hands. In the old days he would never have remembered anyone's name.

Now what?

The line behind is leaning curiously forward.

"We've got records for you to sign," says Jean, sliding hers across the table.

The men smile indulgently. Yoshi nods without surprise, then pushes aside the cellophane on the upper corner. It's funny to see him write with this commonplace, felt-tipped pen.

"To Jean," he scribbles. "My Piano Cake friend. Love Yoshi." He makes a quick elaboration.

"This is my name in *Chinese*, if you have Chinese boyfriend."

She won't blush. Women standing nearby crane their necks to see the inscription. Someone repeats it aloud, and it is passed down the line.

Next he takes Colette's record and inscribes it exactly the same way, only botches the spelling of friend.

When this is over there is an awkward moment where they can either shake hands and bid goodbye – or wait for something else.

Jean has been watching closely. Nothing was exchanged: no notes, no whispered confidence, no secret signs.

Yoshi breaks the silence. "Can you stay?" he asks. "We go for lunch, maybe." He looks to his manager for possible holes in the itinerary. Nicky shrugs his shoulders.

"It can be arranged."

"So?" says Yoshi. "Is settled?"

Jean makes a show of checking with Colette. Her sister's face is drained of colour.

"All right, we'll hang around."

"Just fifteen or twenty minutes," he urges, then looks at the oversized watch on his wrist. He never used to wear a watch.

As they press through the gathering, the women all stare, wondering. Colette sinks onto the little step leading to International Folk Music.

"I'm not feeling so good."

"What do you mean?" Jean is right there.

"I should have got more sleep. Everything feels so unreal." She drops her head between her legs.

Grateful for the distraction, Jean begins to massage her sister's neck and shoulders, running her fingers over the knobs of tension.

"That feels great," Colette moans.

"What do you think's going to happen?" asks Jean.

"Who knows? Did you bring any birth control?"

"What?" Jean's hands freeze. "Why?"

The shoulders rise and fall. "I just have the feeling we're going to go full circle."

Jean sinks to the stair. She feels Colette's tension in her hands now. "I'd keep the baby," she says.

And that's it, of course, the remaining dream. He need never know.

Twenty minutes later, Jean, Colette, Yoshi, and entourage pile into a waiting limo: a plush sedan with a velvet interior and a uniformed driver.

During the short ride to the restaurant Jean feels herself wedged against Yoshi's hip. She wonders if he notices, if he remembers other rides, other occasions of her nearness.

Or have they been replaced and overshadowed by so many new ones?

He puts an arm around her shoulder, and she leans forward to see where his other arm rests. A mirror view; an arm drapes over each sister's shoulder.

Up front, Nicky gives instructions to the driver. "Make a right on Pender. That's it – past that alley."

He consults a sheet of scribbled directions.

Jean takes a long look at Yoshi's face. "You look exactly the same to me," she says.

He smiles sadly and squeezes her shoulder. "You think so – but I am old inside."

He looks straight at her, then Colette. "I feel so tired all the time – and I think too much of death."

Death? The word sounds all wrong in his mouth.

Nicky and the other managers exchange looks. Jean wonders if they have heard this before.

Abruptly Yoshi changes mood. "How old are you now?"

Colette answers. "I'm twenty-three and Jean's twenty-two."

"I don't believe it!" he exclaims, and Jean feels a hand squeeze her shoulder.

Nicky laughs and says, "That's my age."

Yoshi displays exaggerated shock.

"You mean I have been working with you, taking you seriously all this time? That is bad."

Everyone laughs with relief.

As they step out of the car Jean whispers to her sister, "Don't tell him, Colette."

"What?"

"Don't tell him I know."

At the restaurant, a big Chinese place with papier mâché dragons on the wall, Yoshi manoeuvres the assembly so he is sitting between the two sisters. The entourage has expanded to include more men from the local music community. They walk in with hands outstretched and hearty smiles widening their faces.

"Yoshi, you look wonderful!"

Yoshi, Yoshi: they love saying his name. Once, eight years ago, he said to them almost sadly, "Nobody calls me 'Mr. Takahashi' in North America. Always 'Yoshi'."

Lunch is dim sum: dozens of little steaming dishes that he snatches off passing trolleys.

"This one is good!"

A sausage thing lands on Jean's plate, and she prods at it suspiciously.

Yoshi notices. "You think it is something sexy?" Then he pinches the sausage with his own chopsticks and swallows it whole.

She laughs, but already his attention darts elsewhere. The men's talk is full of spirited references to world travel, to changes in personnel at "top levels" of various orchestras, to such and such a virtuoso's cutting his hand while jigging for cod ("He deserved it!"), to who commands what fees.

Colette and Jean continue to munch on the food and end up talking to each other and Nicky the new manager.

There's no hope of getting Yoshi alone, Nicky divulges. Each moment is charted, for months and even years ahead.

He shows them the schedule, a spiral-bound book with a page per day. Nicky's neat handwriting covers most of the space. "I even block in free time," he says, without irony. Colette fills his tea cup. "But there is none at all today. After this we catch a plane."

But there was time before, thinks Jean. And if Colette were alone?

Even the luncheon has been carefully arranged, except for the accident of their appearance. Restaurant and guests were notified well in advance. She finds herself feeling guilty for disrupting the scheduling harmony.

"I guess that's why he never married," says Jean. "No time."

Nicky doesn't respond.

I shouldn't have said that, thinks Jean. Recovering, she quickly asks a question.

"How does he live like this?"

"By remaining very centred," the young man says. "He's right there with all his concentration when he needs to be, and when he doesn't need to be his eyes glaze over."

"Yeah, I remember that."

What can she say? "Do you still like to drink cognac, Yoshi?" Or how about, "What colour is the door to your apartment?"

Jean tries to catch his eye, but he stays just out of range. He bobs in and out of the conversation, listening intently to certain anecdotes, then tuning out as he discovers a new kind of dumpling.

Colette, on his other side, speaks in a confidential tone: "It's been a while, Yoshi . . . " but before she can complete the statement a portly man from the musicians' union executive bursts into noisy laughter. Yoshi looks up, chopsticks poised in mid-air.

"What is joke?"

The man, delighted at having the guest of honour's attention, tells a story about Isaac Stern taking a late plane to Chicago and being forced to circle over the city for three hours. Every twenty minutes the plane passed over the concert hall and he looked down to see hundreds of tiny people pouring in to see him.

"Knowing I-saac, you can *imagine!*" the man guffaws.

Suddenly the lunch is over, and Yoshi springs to his feet, wiping his mouth with a napkin.

"I must go now to Los Angeles. Right, Nicky?" He smiles proudly. "See — I remember."

As Nicky settles the bill, Yoshi shakes hands with the men at the table and finally turns to Colette and Jean.

"Maybe I see you again — some day."

He gives them each a bear hug and rakes their hair affectionately.

"Goodbye, Yoshi."

He pauses a moment and grins at them. "You look so good, you know. Very much like women now."

They flank him as he heads toward the waiting limousine. Just before he climbs into the back seat he turns to Jean, his face creased with concern.

"I hope you still like me," he says in a low voice. His hand reaches for her shoulder and squeezes tightly.

Jean meets his gaze and nods once.

The moon face relaxes, and he turns away, tosses his satchel over his shoulder, and steps into the car. There is a "click". One of the men has snapped a photograph of the departing pianist.

At the end of the block, as the limo gears down to take the corner, Yoshi twists in his seat and sends them a final, two-fisted salute.

"Well, that's that," says Jean.

Colette is quiet beside her. The street is suddenly empty. They walk down Pender to the New Cameo Hotel and head for the bar. Inside, the darkness hits them like an eclipse.

"Two Scotch, no ice."

"You all right?" asks Colette when the drinks arrive.

"Stop asking me that," says Jean. "I'm not an invalid."

The bar is nearly empty. A lone salesman straddles a stool and cradles his rye and ginger. His sample bag is wedged between his feet.

"He didn't let on for a moment," begins Colette, skimming a finger over the rim of her glass.

"That's right." Jean cuts her off.

I hope you still like me. That moon face.

"He looked tired," Colette tries again.

Jean drains her Scotch and sinks into the banquette. She feels her old body disappear into the gauzy upholstery.

His head swinging back and forth. I am old inside.

"No wonder they're going to China," says Jean aloud.

Her sister stares at her, puzzled. Her eyes are just getting used to the dark.

◻

It is the story of an old traveller, Namikoshi, who is tired and sick and falls onto the pathway of the mountain. He must have water, but is too weak to crawl to the stream that he can hear gurgling beyond the bush. Another traveller happens by and, brushing his dirty kimono sleeve out of the way, holds water to the thirsty man's lips.

In the play we traded parts, and hot sake was substituted for water. No one bothered about us drinking: Sam thought it was a kind of Japanese ginger ale and we never told.

   . . . then as a dream
The ragged stranger disappeared.

Days later, Namikoshi falls again on the path:

Feeling deep sadness in his breast,
For he would never, like the bat,

Feel sunlight again,
Nor feel the breath of morning's breeze
Cross his cheek.

Along comes the ragged stranger again and, by simple compassion, rouses Namikoshi. He presses the special *sanri* acupuncture points on his buttocks and calves so the energy begins to flow.

"Thank you, I'll have another glass . . . it is so warming."

This goes on several times, until Namikoshi cries:

"Who is he?
Who is the benevolent stranger?
I must know his name.
His eyes shoot into mine
Like hot arrows . . . "

The second traveller replies:

"Perhaps there are no strangers,
Only relations from past lives
That seek out old—acquaintances."

"Who are you??"

It works out, through a complicated network of revelation, that the stranger is Okakura, Namikoshi's dead brother. Namikoshi is supposed to have killed Okakura in a fit of jealous rage years ago. As penance, he took to the road in search of his punishment. Of course, the long search becomes the punishment.

"I am not yet Okakura—I am
But his ghost shaped by the sound
Of your prayers."

"I don't know whether to fear
Or love you, ghost.

If you are Okakura, how
Should I know you are *you*
And not some Spirit-Pretender?"

Okakura proves his identity by referring to a secret pledge
they made as children. During the enactment of this pledge,
Namikoshi cries out his misdeed and begs forgiveness.
Okakura shakes off his ghost's skin and stands before his
brother looking as he did twenty years ago. He has been
released by the confession. "Say nothing, for one thing is
clear," cries Okakura, his voice wrenched with love.

"You killed me only in your dreams,
And banished yourself to a life
Of celibacy and endless travel
For no reason!
The dream of Okakura forgives you,
While the fleshly Okakura walks
The soil yet!"

"But you said you were my brother's ghost!"

"A ghost only through your one eye.
Open the other wide and see . . . "

Namikoshi obeys; they fall into one another's arms,
weeping. That's how we wrote it and that's how we played
it.

By the end of the bottle we became long-lost brothers.

Epilogue

"And now I'm going to play you an excerpt from Phillip Glass's work. This is called 'Einstein on the Beach'."

Jean turns off the microphone and switches on the stereo system. There is the usual crackling of dust and static before the record begins.

Then the trancelike rhythm fills the auditorium.

She sits on a chair and listens with them.

A big crowd today. At least fifty, with six or seven wheeled in on stretchers from the adjoining hospital. One of these, dressed in a pink bedjacket, is Mrs. Sky, the chunky Pole, who had a slight stroke while Jean was in Victoria. She lies gamely propped up on a hill of pillows and, when Jean looks her way, lifts a triumphant arm.

As the music continues, expressions range from perplexed to nodding sleep. Mrs. Kahn perches on the edge of her chair, arms straddling her cane. Her dress is twinkling with bright yellow sunflowers. She looks like a tiny garden wedged in an East Side tenement block. The old woman stares straight into Jean's eyes and nods once, slowly.

"Next week I'm going to bring in some African and Indian music so you can hear where all this comes from."

This announcement is greeted with sceptical looks.

As Jean packs up she sees Mrs. Kahn beckoning. Tucking records and notes under her arm, she flops on an empty chair beside the old woman.

"Hi," she says.

"You are doing much better now," says Mrs. Kahn. "I think you like teaching us this Music Appreciation. You really feel it."

She waves at the records. "I don't know what this stuff is about, but that is good. You make us want to learn."

Jean smiles. "Thanks, I hope so."

The others are crowding around now, interrupting.

"How is your trip, Professor Hopper? And your family? Did you tell them about us?"

"Sure!"

As always, they reach out and touch her, testing the fabric of her new shirt, venturing opinions.

"Why do you not play us Mahler or Schubert?"

"Maybe I will."

"See — she says she will." A satisfied nod. "Later."

"What happened to that nice boy you introduced us to, the artist?"

"Reuben?"

"Yes, Mr. Reuben. Tell him to come and visit us."

"I'll ask him," promises Jean. "In fact I'll be seeing him this evening."

"Ah — he's your *boyfriend*."

"A little bit," Jean acknowledges.

"A little bit, she says!" This is greeted with roars of laughter.

"Help!" Jean sinks her head for an instant on Mrs. Kahn's hefty shoulder. The material of the old woman's dress nearly blinds her.

Mrs. Kahn starts to chuckle. "Look at you. You're not afraid of me any more."

Jean starts. It's true.

She'd been too dazzled by the nest of sunflowers.

□

We crouched near the row of raspberry bushes. Colette had scooped out a little pit in the dirt and lined it with stones. A wooden lid was disguised with dirt and grass.

"Put the candle in the hole," she directed. "With matches. Then fold the message under it and put the lid back. Make sure no one sees you."

"Then what?"

"At midnight I sneak back here and dig up your note."

"You wouldn't dare!"

"Sure I would. I want to see what you've written for me. Don't forget your code sheet."

I bit the pencil stub and thought and thought. What would I write?

It was after supper, and most of the children were inside, except for some big boys who were slamming a hockey puck against the garage door. They didn't see me.

I lined the piece of cardboard up against the sheet of paper. The cardboard had lots of little rectangles cut in it.

I filled in each hole with block letters.

"Beware," I began, then thought some more. It was almost scary, crouched alone by the bushes in the rapidly descending darkness.

```
When      you      read
      this   I   won't
be      here.      I'm
         lying
              snug
in   bed          staring
   out      the         window
   at
      the        moon.
```

I checked. There was a moon: a slightly dented saucer gleaming over the rooftops.

"Don't forget to put out the candle," I printed. Then I grinned, imagining.

"I'm lying here *right now* thinking of you reading this!"

I drew a little spider at the bottom, my signature. I'd got to the end of the code sheet—no more holes to fill in. So I slid it off, then filled the blank parts of the page with words, anything that came to my head: parakeet, stormy, felt, lesson, creep, before, sky, and dozens more. Then I folded the note and stuck it in the bottom of the hole. I replaced the candle and slid the lid on top. I stood up and kicked some more camouflage over it. It blended right in. I tiptoed home. No one was following me.

We hadn't met him yet.